I0761311

The Death at Awahi

The Death at Awahi

a novel

Harold Burton Meyers

Texas Tech University Press

This book is typeset in Dante. The paper used in this book meets the minimum requirements of ANSI/NISO Z39.48-1992 (R1997). ♾

Designed by Jennifer E. Holmes

Library of Congress Cataloging-in-Publication Data
Meyers, Harold Burton, 1924-
The death at Awahi / Harold Burton Meyers.
p. cm.
Summary: "In the 1920s a young U.S. Indian Service teacher and his wife, a USIS nurse, are posted to a remote New Mexico pueblo and must battle government policies to win over a wary people. Then a killing creates an ethical dilemma that threatens the couple's hopes and Awahi's ancient culture"—Provided by publisher.
ISBN-13: 978-0-89672-599-7 (hardcover : alk. paper)
ISBN-10: 0-89672-599-5 (hardcover : alk. paper)
1. Pueblo Indians—New Mexico—Fiction. I. Title.
PS3563.E898D43 2007
813'.54—dc22
2006022577

Printed in the United States of America
07 08 09 10 11 12 13 14 15/ 9 8 7 6 5 4 3 2 1
TS

This is a novel and should be read as such. No pueblo like Awahi exists or has existed, except in the author's imagination. The same applies to characters, ceremonies, customs, traditions, history, language, and incidents. Gallup, New Mexico, does exist, and so once did John Collier, the American Indian Defense Association, and the U.S. Indian Service's controversial "Christianize and civilize" policy.

Texas Tech University Press
Box 41037
Lubbock, Texas 79409-1037 USA
800.832.4042
ttup@ttu.edu
www.ttup.ttu.edu

To J.A.M., as always

The Death at Awahi

Chapter 1

The Model T Ford skidded to a stop in a mudhole on the dirt road that a few years later would become famous as U.S. Route 66. The rear wheels dug in to the hubs, spinning, going nowhere. Gasoline fumes poured into the car. The motor sputtered and died.

"Engine's flooded," Quill said. "Nothing to do but wait for somebody to pull us out."

"We're all alone out here," Jane said.

"Somebody's bound to come along."

"Who? When?"

"I don't know. Somebody, sometime."

"And we just wait?"

"If nobody turns up by morning, I'll walk back to the state line. It can't be more than five miles or so."

Darkness settled over the sagebrush flats like a lid coming down. Distant mesas and buttes faded into a starless void. Coyotes mourned all around. Wind flapped the car's canvas top and side curtains.

"I'm freezing," Jane said.

Quill reached into the jumble of boxes and suitcases in the rear seat to pull out a quilt. He tucked it around her.

"That better?"

"That little store at the state line had tourist cabins in back. We should have stopped there."

"I didn't know the road would be this bad."

"You could have asked."

"I did ask. Fellow in the store said we'd be able to make it to Gallup before dark with time to spare."

Feeling around in the back again, he found the thermos.

"There's still coffee. Probably not real hot, but warm."

He poured a cup. She folded mittened hands around it and breathed in the faint suggestion of steam. He poured a cup for himself. There were no lights anywhere and nothing to hear but wind and coyotes.

Jane began to cry.

"If you'd kept your mouth shut at that damned meeting, we wouldn't be here," she said. "But no, you had to rock the boat."

It was not what he expected to hear from her. She seldom swore and was far more inclined than he to rock boats. He was the cautious one, always willing to seek common ground, always eager to dodge a confrontation. When she felt something was wrong, she said so straight out—chin up, arms akimbo, fearlessly. Years before she was old enough to cast a ballot she had marched with suffragettes in West Texas for the right of women to vote. Twice she had been arrested, and word of her rambunctious past had nearly kept her from being accepted for nurse's training.

Sounding more like her feisty self, no longer crying, she said, "It wouldn't be so bad if you'd stuck to your guns and said what you really think. But, no, you had to be Mr. Milquetoast. Why did you speak up at all if you were going to cave in at the first unfriendly word?"

"I didn't cave in."

"I say you did. You knew that fat idiot was spouting nonsense when he told us our job was to Christianize and civilize the children. Make them forget they're Indians, he said, and punish any kids you catch speaking their own language—their own language, for God's sake! But when you got up to object you couldn't bear not being one of the boys. So you caved in."

"Don't forget, that fat idiot was the U.S. commissioner of Indian affairs, the guy we work for, and the nonsense he was peddling has been official U.S. policy for fifty years. And I didn't just stand up on my own. He asked why I was shaking my head. I had to answer. And I told him why. I pointed out what we all knew but nobody would say—that the English-only policy has never done anything but create problems."

"That's not the way it was. You started yes-sirree-bobbing right away, just like any Old Turk in the place, before you even made your argument. I was there too, remember? All you managed to do was get everybody but me down on you."

"You're not down on me? I hadn't noticed."

She ignored the interruption. "And now we're being punished for it—buried in mud with no place to go but just about the worst Indian school in the whole country."

"I don't see being transferred to Awahi as punishment. It's an opportunity, a promotion, a chance to get ahead faster than I'd ever hoped to."

"Opportunity? Promotion? Awahi?"

"Ordinarily I wouldn't even be considered for a principal's job without another five or ten years of teaching, as you very well know. And we won't be at Awahi forever."

"It'll be forever or no job at all, from everything I've heard."

Quill tried to put his arm around her. Jane pushed him away. She had never done that before.

"We were doing so well at Phoenix," she said. "You liked your job. I loved mine. We were saving some money. I thought we were all set to start a family. Now we're stuck in a mudhole in the middle of nowhere and worrying before we even get there about how long we'll be able to keep our jobs. It'll be years, if ever, before we have a baby."

"I just want to be sure we can take good care of one. It won't be too long, I promise. We'll have our baby."

"Not at Awahi," she said. "Not ever at Awahi."

They munched on bread and cheese from the food box, washing it down with the last of the lukewarm coffee. For the first time Quill could remember, they ate without talking. He could think of nothing to say that she would want to hear.

Beside him in the Model T but a thousand miles away, Jane curled up on her seat, wrapped in the quilt. He dug out another one for himself and sat upright behind the wheel, too long-legged to find a comfortable position. The wind and coyotes howled. Neither he nor Jane fell asleep for hours.

Dawn stilled the coyotes and the wind died to a breeze, but dark clouds hid the sun. Two Indian men wearing broad-brimmed black hats with stovepipe crowns showed up with a team of horses and a length of heavy rope. They waded through the mud to bargain with Quill, using sign language and a few Spanish and English words. He passed over fifty cents and half a loaf of bread from the food box. The two Indians backed the horses into the mudhole and tied the rope to the axle. With a jerk and a tilt, the Model T came out of the mud and rolled to solid ground. Jane slept through it all—the jerk, the tilt, and the gasping roar of the motor as Quill cranked it to life.

Chapter 2

Quill wrestled the mud-spattered Model T out of the ruts of the future Route 66 toward a roadside structure that had once been painted white. A faded sign proclaimed:

PARSON'S STORE
GROCERIES GAS CURIOS
GALLUP'S FINEST

The porch roof jutted over the driveway like the bill of Babe Ruth's cap, affording a patch of dry ground in front of the store. Quill stopped the car next to the porch, on which sat a steel barrel marked "GAS" and a green and white pump topped by a clear glass cylinder. A strip of numbers from one to ten ran down the glass, marking gallons.

Jane poked her head out of her quilt cocoon. With her coppery hair cut short and tousled, she looked like a sleepy-eyed child.

"Where are we?"

"Outskirts of Gallup."

Unsnapping the window curtain and pushing it aside, Quill eased himself out of the car feet first, over a running board loaded with suitcases, boxes, and a five-gallon gasoline can, all but the gas can covered by a muddy tarp. Jane scooted across the seat and held out her arms. Quill reached in and swung her out. She wore brown riding breeches, leather leggings, and a white Hudson's Bay coat with one black and two green stripes. Given the bulkiness of his mackinaw and her coat, he could barely get his arms around her. He kissed her ear before putting her down.

She leaned her head against his chest as her feet touched the ground. "I'm sorry," she said. "I was awful last night."

"You were scared and worried and cold besides," he said.

Jane started toward a privy behind the store just as a sharp-nosed man in overalls and a stained sheepskin coat came out of the store and stood by the gas pump.

"Hey, young fella," he called, "we got a inside toilet, if'n you want."

Jane turned back.

"Right through there, son," the sharp-nosed man said, gesturing at the door behind him. "Got city water now. Septic tank, but city water."

"City water," Quill said. "That's surprising, out here at the edge of town."

"Ain't it, though? For a old coal and railroad burg, Gallup's getting right up to date. If they'd bring the sewer line and pavement out this far I'd finally make it all the way into the twentieth century, only twenty-three years late."

Jane went up the steps, smiling. The man looked sharply at her and then stepped back to hold the door.

"Welcome to Gallup, miss," he said.

"You got gas in that tank?" Quill asked.

"All you want."

"We've fought mud all the way from Holbrook. Low gear a lot of the time, sucking up gas. Been running on fumes the last ten, twenty miles."

"You didn't fill at the state line? At Sanders or Lupton?"

Quill sensed criticism. "Stopped, but no gas. Truck hasn't been able to get through since the roads thawed, they said."

"Don't wonder. Old Man Braddock, he's the gas distributor, he don't send his truck out when the roads is like this. Don't pay, he says. Tears up the equipment."

The man inserted a key into a padlock on the gas-pump handle.

"Nuisance," he said. "Got to keep everything locked up tight. Coal miners is out on strike again and times so hard they'll steal anything that ain't nailed down right before your eyes and think it's their due. Old Wobblies, most of them, and Bohunks too."

Quill reached into the car and turned off the motor. "Left it running, case you didn't have gas either. I'm not fond of cranking any more than I have to. Known too many men to break an arm when the engine kicked back."

He leaned in through the window to tip the front seat cushion forward onto the floor, uncovering the gas tank. He unscrewed the cap.

"How many gallons, you reckon?" the store man asked.

Quill took a measuring stick from its resting place among the upended cushion's spherical springs and poked it in the tank. When he pulled it out, barely an eighth of an inch showed wet.

"Right on nine and a half or a bit more, I expect," he said. "But I used up my extra can of gas, too, so that'll make it just short of fifteen altogether."

"You was cutting it close, all right," the man said, pumping pink gasoline into the glass cylinder.

"Like I said, down to fumes. Couldn't help it. Car's heavily loaded, and we bogged down half a dozen times. Spent last night this side of the state line, buried to the hubs in a mudhole, all four wheels. Couldn't dig out before dark. Couple of Indians came along this morning and pulled us out."

"I know the hole," the man said. "State fills it up every so often, but them two Navajos dig it right out again. They got a good thing going there—go out every morning to see what they caught. I don't know how many Navvies that there mudhole is feeding."

"Well, I was surely glad to see them turn up with that team. Made me miss the old horse-and-buggy days."

"Maybe," the man said. "But I been bogged down behind six mules many a time."

Quill doubted the aspersion on mule power. He had spent much of his boyhood with reins around his neck and his hands on a plow, staring at the rear end of a mule, breaking sun-baked soil on the hardscrabble Texas homestead his family had moved to from Tennessee when he was not yet ten. He had a deep appreciation for what a mule could do, if it wanted to.

The glass cylinder was pink to the top. The man on the porch unhooked the pump's hose and leaned down to hand Quill the nozzle.

"Where you headed?"

"Awahi." Quill poked the nozzle into the tank. The level of pink gasoline in the cylinder began to drop, gallon by gallon.

"You the new principal down there? Taking old Wilman's place?"

Quill shifted the nozzle to his left hand and reached his right hand up toward the man. "That's right. My name's Thompson—Quill Thompson."

The man wiped his hand on the leg of his overalls before leaning down to shake.

"Pleased," he said. "Jim Parsons. Be glad to have your trade, Mr. Thompson, should you see fit."

"I'm sure you'll see us from time to time, Mr. Parsons."

"Hell of a time of year to be going to Awahi—February. Too bad Wilman couldn't hold on a few more months. Awahi ain't never no treat, I reckon, but it's bound to be nicer in the spring, except for the wind and sandstorms, of course."

"I don't mind. A promotion for me, and my wife'll be opening a clinic."

"A clinic?"

"She's a nurse."

"That little thing's a nurse? I first seen her, I thought she was your daughter."

"She'll be pleased to hear that," Quill said, saying what he knew the man wanted to hear, but also knowing that neither he nor the storekeeper was anywhere near the truth. The storekeeper had thought she was a boy, not his daughter, and either way it would not please Jane to hear it. Both he and Jane had grown up dirt poor in Texas, though her people had once owned a ranch and his had always farmed somebody else's land. She had fought too long and worked too hard for her nurse's cap to appreciate being taken for a child of either sex.

Quill topped off the tank.

"I make it a touch or two over nine and a half gallons," Parsons said. "You was sure enough near to burning air."

Parsons pumped gas again, up to the five-gallon mark, still talking. "The way I hear it, he was lucky to stay out of jail and keep his job. Wilman, I mean. At least, that's what folks say."

"I wouldn't know about that," Quill said, which in an official sense was true, though rumors had spread throughout the U.S. Indian Service that his predecessor at Awahi Pueblo had been publicly accused of defrauding the government by illegally diverting clothes and food to a mission school. The man had escaped prosecution but not punishment. He was demoted from principal to teacher and transferred to Pine Ridge, headquarters for the Ogallala Sioux reservation in South Dakota, there to serve out the remaining years before he could retire on a pension.

To employees of the U.S. Indian Service like Quill and Jane, Pine Ridge was known as a miserable hellhole far from any town on a treeless plain where the wind always blew and poverty-stricken Indians were more inclined to celebrate the slaughter of Custer's troops at Little Big Horn than the Fourth of July. But it was also said in the Indian Service that Pine Ridge wasn't really that much worse than Awahi. The wind blew just as hard at Awahi as it did at Pine Ridge, the road to it was just as rough and primitive, and the people just as destitute and hostile. The Awahi didn't have Little Big Horn to brag about, of course, but they did have the great rebellion of 1680, when Awahi joined other pueblos from Taos to Zuñi in a massacre of their Spanish occupiers. Peaceful as the tribe appeared to be, newcomers to Awahi were always warned to be on their guard lest the populace try to reenact 1680.

Parsons kept talking about Wilman.

"Lot of folks got themselves rich out to Awahi over the years, or so I'm told," he said. "Half the goods sent there went God knows where and nobody to say 'em nay. Poor old Wilman, I guess he got greedy or careless, one or t'other, and let hisself get caught. Hell of it is, the missionary who got the stuff, he walked away with no mud on his boots. Or so I hear."

Quill made no reply. He filled his five-gallon can with pink gasoline.

"'Course, I hear it weren't the first time Wilman got out of line. Folks say that's how come he got sent to Awahi in the first place, years ago. Happens all the time, folks say. When some up-and-coming feller like Wilman was then or maybe like you are now messes up, Washington sends him some place at the end of the world like Awahi and forgets about him till he stubs his toe again. Then it's Pine Ridge or no job at all. Or so folks say. Or maybe you don't see it that way?"

Quill said nothing.

After a pause, Parsons continued. "Funny thing. I never knowed his name. The missionary who turned on Wilman, I mean. Only thing I ever heard him called was 'the missionary,' though there's others at Awahi."

"Just 'the missionary'? That's all?"

"That's all. Fella to stay away from, all I hear. Seems like a friend, a fine Christian gent, and then knifes you in the back, or so folks say. I hear that's what he done to poor Wilman. He got all those clothes and things for his mission and then blowed the whistle on him. 'Course, other folks say, no, that ain't the way it were. Wilman didn't give nobody government property. He sold it at give-away prices and pocketed the change, thank you, ma'am. Besides, these same folks say, it was a entire other mission school Wilman was selling government property to, not the missionary's school. When Wilman wouldn't cut him in on the deal, that was when the missionary went to Fort Frazier and spilled the beans, or so folks say."

Parsons put a finger alongside his nose, sealing off one nostril while he blew through the other. He wiped his finger on his pants leg, sighing.

"Don't know who to believe no more," he said. "Maybe nobody."

Quill still said nothing.

"I seen him now and again—the missionary, I mean. Looks like Custer or maybe Kit Carson. Long yellow hair, down to his shoulders, getting a little gray now, and real bright eyes—greenish blue like them flames that dance over a hot fire that's just been coaled. You see his eyes and you think there must be a fire in his skull. Scorch your skin, his eyes will. And talk? Get him going, he'll talk your arm off. Watch him, though. Don't let him stand close to you when he starts on religion. He gets excited, grabs you by the shirt, sticks his face in yours and shouts Hell and damnation. BANG! BANG! BANG! Right in your ear. Last time he done that to me my head had bells in it for a week. Had to wipe spit off'n my face."

The pump's glass cylinder was empty.

"Tell you one other thing," Parsons said, "though I maybe hadn't ought. Damnedest missionary I ever heard of. Every now and again he'll turn up here in town, down on Railroad Avenue, where the action is, if you know where to look. Plays poker day and night for a while, or so I'm told, and mostly wins, especially the big pots. And when he rakes it in, he'll say, 'Thank you, gentlemen, for your contribution to the Lord's good work.' Likes the Railroad Avenue girls, too, or so folks say, and not just to preach to. Don't know what he says to 'em when he pulls up his pants."

He added: "Was I you I'd watch that bird like he was a rattler in the corner."

* * *

Parsons allowed them to use his back room to make themselves presentable before they started for Fort Frazier to report for duty at Awahi. Jane put on a high-necked white shirtwaist and a full black skirt, longer than she generally preferred these days. She tamed her tousled hair and hid most of it under a hat that Quill thought looked like a helmet. She said it was the latest style.

"Do I look like a respectable married woman?" she asked, trying to check her hemline without a long mirror as she pulled on white gloves.

"You'd fool anyone," Quill said.

He dressed in a starched white shirt, a clean celluloid collar, and his good blue suit, unbothered by the fact that it was wrinkled from being folded in a suitcase. Jane helped him knot the red-and-blue-striped tie he had worn when they were married. He put it on only for state occasions. Watching in the small mirror over the sink as Jane tightened the knot, Quill thought his throat rising from the stiff collar looked as scrawny as the plucked neck of a turkey gobbler.

Finally he put on his high-top dress shoes, polished to a high gloss. Made of supple kangaroo leather from Australia, they conformed to the shape of his feet as the heavy work shoes he usually wore did not. He had grown up barefooted, the youngest of twelve children, and had not had a pair of shoes of his own until he went to Fort Worth to live with his oldest brother and enter high school—the first member of his family to go past the fourth grade, let alone the eighth. He still found most shoes confining. He liked to say that his kangaroo-hide shoes, which he ordered out of the Monkey Ward catalog, cost an arm and leg but fit like his own skin.

Quill lifted Jane into the car over the loaded running board and got in himself. Before he could snap the side curtain into place, Parsons leaned in to say that they would be on gravel all the way to Fort Frazier.

"Ain't far and no mud," he said. "You won't have no trouble at all."

He was right. When they arrived at Fort Frazier, Quill crawled out of the Model T and stepped onto a brick sidewalk with not a speck on his kangaroo shoes.

Chapter 3

The offices at the Fort Frazier Agency occupied a thick-walled sandstone relic of Indian-fighting days. Quill's shoes squeaked down the heavily oiled wooden floors of the central hall, disturbing a silence so absolute that it seemed to have been accumulating for decades. He tried tiptoeing, but with each step mousy sounds echoed through what appeared to be an unoccupied building. The frosted glass windows of the doors opening off the hall bore no names, only numbers. Whispering, Jane wondered why.

"Names change, numbers don't," Quill said. "Saves a lot of trouble as people come and go."

At the end of the hall door No. 1 had a name on it:

Mr. E. R. Thornton
SUPERINTENDENT

Mr. E. R. Thornton was an elderly gentleman in a well-pressed black suit. He was slight and fragile looking, a foot shorter than Quill. Greeting them with a soft Virginia accent and a courtly, if distant, manner, Mr. Thornton invited them to have a seat and inquired courteously but without curiosity about their trip. He then made it clear that he had little interest in them or in the day-to-day affairs of the Awahi Pueblo. He left Awahi to his deputy superintendent, he said.

On learning, however, that Jane was to set up a clinic at Awahi, he leaned forward, elbows on his desk, and jabbed the air with a monogrammed silver letter opener. "No one informed me of that," he said, and complained of Washington's growing indifference to traditional protocols and procedures.

He concluded the meeting by sending Jane across a grassy quadrangle to the medical director's office at the agency hospital. Quill he directed down the hall to his deputy, Mr. Lasher, whose office door identified him only as No. 2.

"Ah," Mr. Lasher said, ducking his head at Quill but not offering to shake hands. He was a weary-seeming, middle-aged figure in a baggy gray suit, with pomaded hair and teeth that were too white and even to be real. He peered over half-glasses perched on the tip of his nose. Whenever his eyes seemed about to settle on Quill, they flicked away. "You're the new man at Awahi."

"Yes, sir." Quill handed over his orders.

"Ah. You were supposed to be here yesterday? Thursday? This is Friday. Took a day of leave, perhaps?"

"No, sir," Quill said. "Weather. The roads."

"Ah. So. I'll take care of it. I anticipate no difficulty in allowing you the extra day. Mrs. Thompson will have to discuss the matter with the medical director, of course, but I shall mention to him that we are overlooking your lost day and suggest that he might do the same for her."

Mr. Lasher discussed in detail the duties and responsibilities that Quill would be undertaking at Awahi. For the most part he spoke in a monotone, as though no one thing he said was more important than anything else. After going over a multitude of details about the school and its curriculum, he discussed the reports of every kind that Quill would be required to file weekly, monthly, and quarterly. These covered everything from daily attendance to the number of pounds of beans used per every ten students in preparing the daily hot lunch. Most were the kinds of report that no one would ever want to look at unless they weren't filed.

Mr. Lasher then turned to Quill's powers as the ranking government official at Awahi and therefore the ruler of an ancient pueblo with its own religion, culture, and customs.

"As the Indian agent at Awahi," Mr. Lasher said, using an obsolete title long since retired because of scandals generated by those who had held it, "you will be responsible not just for the school but for everything that happens at the pueblo, if it affects the federal interest. There is a tribal council and a so-called governor, but he is powerless. You are free to overrule any action that is not in accord with your interpretation of our policies. Don't expect an easy time of it, however—the Awahis have a reputation for docility, but they are in fact an ignorant, dangerous race of thieving, superstitious savages, always bragging about killing conquistadores and priests back in 1680 or thereabouts. Mr. Wilman repeatedly warned that antigovernment feeling is strong among the young bucks, and rising. You should take care about personal safety. Lock doors, don't go out at night, that kind of thing."

Quill asked how many Awahis there were. He had checked the 1920 U.S. Census, but the population figure given for the Awahi enumeration district was only 39. Mr. Lasher said the census taker had not attempted to count Indians, just white residents, including ranch families living on reservation land. No one knew the size of the Indian population.

"It fluctuates—epidemics, malnutrition, et cetera. We generally think in terms of a thousand, perhaps fifteen hundred," Mr. Lasher said. "It's not important."

He added that school enrollment in the six grades at Awahi

also varied a good bit, even within a single school year. However many students signed up at the start of a year, attendance would drop after the children received their clothing allotment—shoes, stockings, undergarments, shirts, pants or dresses, and a sweater for each child. Some children might enroll only for the clothing and move to one of the missionary schools as soon as they got it. In addition, the death rate among children was high, thanks to recurring epidemics of everything from measles to typhoid fever and diphtheria. In the higher grades, students would drop out as they reached fourteen or fifteen to assume their adult roles in the pueblo.

There were four teachers at Awahi, three of whom were young adventure seekers who had come from the Midwest or South to spend a year or two in the Wild West before settling down as housewives back in Muncie or Montgomery. The best that Quill could hope for from these young women, Mr. Lasher said, was that they would show up for work each day more or less on time and not attempt to form inappropriate liaisons with Indian men. He spoke highly of the fourth teacher, Mrs. Wallis, who taught grades four through six, which were small enough to be combined in one class. Mrs. Wallis was an older woman and highly trained—she had a master's degree from Columbia Teachers College, Mr. Lasher reported with awe. She was zealous about drawing the Awahis from their pagan beliefs and was also a stern disciplinarian. She was, in short, he said, someone Quill could rely on. He added that she would without doubt have been promoted to principal had she been a man.

As an aside, he reminded Quill that while it would be up to him to discipline the boys, for reasons of delicacy it was best to designate a woman to punish female students. Fortunately Mrs. Wallis was willing to take on the task—not every woman teacher would—and after one of her whippings, he said, only a very stubborn girl caught speaking Awahi would repeat the offense.

"Who whipped the boys after Mr. Wilman left?" Quill asked.

"Why, Mrs. Wallis, of course," Mr. Lasher said, and went on talking.

At last he asked, "Any questions?"

"A couple," Quill said, "if you don't mind."

Mr. Lasher nodded.

"Why are you making this change at Awahi now, in the middle of the school year?"

Mr. Lasher's eyes drifted toward a window at the right of his desk.

"Ah," he said. "A very sad story. Mr. Wilman was—is—a fine man, an excellent educator, and a skilled administrator. A gentleman of seasoned judgment, with long experience in the Service."

He sighed. Quill sensed unsaid words floating past him: *Not at all like you.*

"Last fall," the assistant superintendent said, "someone at Awahi wrote a letter to Mr. John Collier of the American Indian Defense Association, alleging irregularities at Mr. Wilman's school. As you surely know, Mr. Collier is a severe critic of the Bureau of Indian Affairs. The letter accused Mr. Wilman of illegally passing government property, specifically sweaters, shoes, and other wearing apparel, as well as a large quantity of foodstuffs, to the Reverend Dirk Housma for use at the Reformed Church of the New Beginning mission school. Mr. Collier forwarded the letter to the chairman of the congressional subcommittee that oversees the bureau's appropriation. The chairman sent the letter on to the commissioner, who asked this office to look into the allegations."

Mr. Lasher produced another sigh. He took off his half-glasses and waved them slowly through the air as though directing an orchestra in a dirge.

"We found that food and clothing had indeed been supplied to Reverend Housma but for a good purpose. By providing relief to the needy children enrolled in Reverend Housma's Protestant school, Mr. Wilman was seeking to carry out the aims of the 'Christianize and civilize' policy. We naturally thought that Mr. Thornton's report would put an end to the matter. But in November, when the commissioner appeared at a congressional hearing, the subcommittee chairman—a member of the commissioner's own party!—called it a scandal and accused the bureau of breaking the law, wasting taxpayers' money, and breaching constitutional barriers between church and state. The Washington papers used the chairman's remarks to have a field day at the commissioner's expense. He was obliged to send Mr. Wilman to Pine Ridge to serve until he is eligible for retirement. And you were appointed to take his place at Awahi."

Quill had another question. "Who complained to Mr. Collier?"

"We are not certain. The name was deleted on the copy of the letter sent to us. However, we believe it was a missionary named Thomas Achilles Sandringham Jr., although Mr. Wilman regards Sandringham as a good friend and does not believe he would send such a letter behind his back."

Again Mr. Lasher sighed.

"Unfortunately, in our investigation we learned that Mr. Wilman may be mistaken in his estimation of Reverend Sandringham's character. In his youth Sandringham briefly studied for the ministry but was expelled from the seminary after he was found with a woman from a traveling carnival in his dormitory room. Before coming to Awahi he worked at several disreputable trades and became an itinerant preacher, though we do not believe he was ever ordained in any established church."

"What denomination is he?"

"I scarcely know. I'm told he sometimes refers to himself as a reformed Baptist, which is possible because his father is a distinguished evangelist of that faith in Alabama. Sandringham has also declared himself to be a Mormon, which one doubts because he has no wives."

The corners of Mr. Lasher's mouth twitched. For a moment Quill thought the man was going to smile, but he did not. He only said, "It seems he practices polygamy without marriage." His mouth twitched again before he went on. "He is also the uncle of the war ace Thomas A. Sandringham, who shot down eight Germans in the Great War and is now one of the aviators engaged in exploring the possibility of transcontinental airmail service between Los Angeles and New York. Flies right over Awahi from time to time, I understand. You've surely heard of him?"

Quill shook his head. "Afraid not. But what makes you suspect that Reverend Sandringham blew the whistle on Mr. Wilman?"

"In studying the letter that caused all this difficulty, we noted a striking peculiarity in the writer's style. All the important words and passages were written in capitals. That was true also of letters written by Reverend Sandringham in perpetrating a mail fraud of which he was convicted."

"Mail fraud? Convicted? What was that about?"

"It had something to do with money-raising letters he wrote for Reverend Housma's uncle and predecessor at Awahi. He was accused of keeping the money he raised for himself. Mr. Wilman always felt it was a trumped-up case—a case of interdenominational rivalry, I believe he called it."

Quill had one more question. "Why was I picked to replace Mr. Wilman?"

Mr. Lasher looked at him as though he were an Awahi of a singularly unsavory sort. He tapped a folder on his desk. "You were 'picked,' as you put it, because the commissioner of Indian affairs said he wanted a Young Turk for the job, someone whose appointment would appease John Collier and Congress. Someone like you."

"I don't see myself as a Young Turk, and I've never met John Collier," Quill protested.

"Perhaps not, but you have that reputation. The commissioner said he recalls hearing you attack the Christianize and civilize policy at a meeting in Phoenix last summer. I understand that, contrary to established bureau policy, you even advocated allowing children to speak their native languages in our schools. So you are going to Awahi. Like it or not, you're our Young Turk."

Mr. Lasher seemed to take no pleasure in the thought. He paused, sighed, and polished his glasses. Leaning over the table and for the first time looking directly at Quill, he said: "Whatever your personal opinions, you are expected to dot every i and cross every t in carrying out bureau policy. If you deviate from policy—and given your reputation and the peculiar circumstances of your appointment, we recognize that you are likely to do so and that we may not be able to do much about it—we expect you to keep us informed so that we may be prepared for any backlash. Above all, however, you are to crack down hard, without hesitation, on anything that might give rise to adverse publicity. Just keep in mind that the commissioner wants to hear no more about Awahi, especially not from John Collier, Congress, or the press. Nor do we. Not a word. Not for any reason. So don't rock the boat. That's all we ask. *Don't rock the boat.* Do you understand?"

"Yes, sir, I believe so."

* * *

Dr. Andrews, the medical director, was a haggard-looking man with bushy white eyebrows and many missing teeth, who sipped as he talked from what Jane recognized as a small bottle of medicinal brandy. She encountered no questions about why she was a day late reporting. What she did encounter was astonishment that she had been assigned to establish a clinic at Awahi Pueblo. Like Mr. Thornton, Dr. Andrews had not been informed that a clinic was to be set up. Nor had he been consulted about who should run it. It was hard to tell which oversight offended him more.

Jane's papers were in order, however. She was provided with two boxes of medical supplies from the Fort Frazier Agency hospital's stockroom and a variety of daily, weekly, monthly, and quarterly forms to fill in. Basic equipment for a medical field-office would be shipped to her as soon as possible. She also got authority to hire a handyman and someone to act as a medical assistant and interpreter, if she could find anyone in the local population capable of doing the job.

Everyone she talked to offered sympathy because Awahi was such a terrible place, where the wind never stopped blowing and a hostile native population lived in tight proximity to one another under deplorable sanitary conditions. The villagers resisted every effort at vaccination or hygienic reform, and every few years a killing epidemic of one sort or another swept through the pueblo.

"Just be glad you don't have children," a nurse told Jane.

After lunch at the Employees Club—toasted cheese sandwiches and stewed tomatoes, with a stale cookie for dessert—they set out for Awahi on a muddy road under stormy skies. As they bumped along toward a range of low mountains, Jane said, "I don't think Dr. Andrews or anyone else at Fort Frazier cares a pin about us or Awahi. They're not interested in anything but neat records and no trouble."

"What I got from Mr. Lasher and Mr. Thornton," Quill said, "was that they don't like us or our ideas, but they can't do anything about it right now. So we're on our own until we rock the boat. Then they'll toss us to the sharks."

"That might be better than Awahi," Jane said.

Chapter 4

They saw the sun for the first time that day as they came out of the mountains. Below them the Awahi River sliced through a vast canyon-cut plateau "like a whiplash," as an early explorer reported. In a distant loop of the river, the stacked dwellings of Awahi gleamed in the dying sun's rays. Beyond the pueblo loomed Hawalanee, the flat-topped, sheer-sided dwelling place of Awahi's gods. For a fleeting moment the pueblo might have been the city of gold that Spanish conquistadores had dreamed of finding.

"It looks like a magical place, sort of," Jane said.

It was the first remotely good thing Quill had heard her say about Awahi.

As they wound their way to the valley floor another rainstorm struck. The Model T's headlamps barely cut the darkness. Lightning slashed the night sky. Rain washed in blinding sheets over the windshield. Jane reached over to crank the wiper back and forth so that Quill could make out the water-filled ruts he was trying to follow. With the rain came wind. It howled out of the mountains and down the valley, shaking the side curtains and swaying the car. The rain stopped as they neared Awahi and found their way to the school. The wind did not.

A stone wall enclosed the school compound. An elaborate iron scrollwork sign over the gate spelled out "Fort Awahi" in rusted Spencerian script. Inside the gate the old army structures still stood, though marred by ragtag additions. It was Fort Frazier in degraded miniature, grassless and treeless except for a few ancient cottonwoods along the perimeter. Fort Awahi had been built as a U.S. Cavalry outpost in the 1870s to protect a railroad that a politically well-connected Wall Street speculator proposed to run past Awahi to Los Angeles. The speculator abandoned his plans, and the army its outpost, when another speculator beat him to California by another route. A few years later the army turned the site over to the Interior Department for use as a school.

At first all that Quill and Jane could see in the Model T's lights were tumbleweeds skittering across what had once been the parade ground and coming to rest against the stone wall. In the darkness the buildings were little more than shadows, but Mr. Lasher had given Quill a map of the premises, drawn up by a government surveyor, which gave them some sense of the place.

Jane said, "It looks like everybody died or moved away."

Quill stopped in front of the principal's house, a stone pile that in army days had been the commanding officer's quarters. A porch with stone columns stretched across the front and bay windows flanked the entrance.

"It's huge," Jane said. "A fortress, not a house."

"Mr. Lasher said it's the best house in the Indian Service—walls two feet thick, so it's warm in winter and cool in summer. Lots of rooms and well furnished, he said. The Wilmans had everything refinished and reupholstered."

"It still looks like a fortress."

Leaving the motor running to keep the Ford's headlamps on, Quill unsnapped the door curtain beside him, dropped to the ground, and lifted Jane out. He felt in his pocket for the key he had been given at Fort Frazier. As they started up the walk, a figure materialized on the porch, floating out of darkness into the light.

Quill stopped, took a step backward. Jane clutched his arm.

"Welcome to Awahi, Mr. Thomas. Mrs. Thomas."

"Who are you?"

"Reverend Sandringham, Thomas Achilles Sandringham Jr., pastor of the Church of Jehovah's Sweet Light of Jesus Mission. I am at your service, Mr. Thomas." The voice was low, soft, and Southern.

"Thompson. My name is Thompson."

"But Mrs. Wallis said—"

"I assure you, sir, my name is Thompson."

"I beg your pardon, Mr. Thompson, Mrs. Thompson. I was misinformed. In any case, sir, I am delighted to welcome you and your lady to Awahi and would be pleased to be of service to you."

Quill and Jane could make out little more of him than that he was as tall as Quill, had a clean-shaven chin and shoulder-length hair, and was dressed all in black.

The walls of the house formed an alcove into which a wide door of crisscrossed solid oak planks was set. Quill tried the key Mr. Lasher had given him. It would not turn.

"Damn!" he said.

"It appears, sir, that you may have been given the backdoor key," Reverend Sandringham said. "Perhaps I can help."

He thrust out his hand, opened and closed his fingers a time or two. A key appeared in his palm.

Quill jumped. "Where did that come from?"

"I was a magician before I found Christ and my present calling."

Quill took the key, tried it, and swung the door open.

"How come you have a key?"

"I was—am—a friend of Joshua Wilman and Mrs. Wilman. You are fortunate enough to have running water in your abode. When the Wilmans left they asked me to keep a banked fire in the kitchen range to avoid having the pipes freeze." He handed the key to Quill.

"I'd have thought someone on the school staff might have tended the fire," Quill said.

"I take it you have not met your school staff?" Reverend Sandringham said.

"Meaning?"

"I believe it is possible, sir, that Mr. Wilman did not have a high opinion of the staff's reliability."

The house was warm but dark. Swirling his cloak about, Reverend Sandringham snapped his fingers, summoning a lighted match. A kerosene lamp stood on a hall table. He lifted its chimney and touched the match to the wick. In its light Quill caught a glimpse of hollowed-out cheeks, gray-streaked golden hair, and blue green eyes that shone so brightly they seemed to emit more light than they gathered in.

With Sandringham's help it took only a couple of trips to carry in what was needed for the night.

"We'll leave the rest till morning," Quill said.

"I wouldn't do that. These people don't care who owns what. When they see something they want, they take it."

"We'll chance it."

As Sandringham left he seized Quill's hand and held it. "Brother Thompson," he said, "have you FOUND CHRIST? Are you a CHRISTIAN?"

Startled, Quill said, "I was brought up a Methodist."

"Ah, but are you a CHRISTIAN?" The missionary put his face inches from Quill's. "THINK, Brother Thompson, THINK!

Methodism means no more than putting on a suit and tie. The question is, HAVE YOU FOUND CHRIST? Have you TAKEN HIM INTO YOUR HEART? Are you ONE WITH HIM?"

Quill pushed him out the door and toured the house with Jane. Mr. Lasher had been right. In room after room the furniture was oak, recently refurbished, and comfortable.

"We've got so much room we could put up your whole family," Jane said.

"God forbid," he said. His eleven siblings had provided him with forty nieces and nephews. He was also well supplied with aunts and uncles and first and second cousins.

* * *

Quill was up well before dawn the next morning. He liked to rise at 5:00 a.m. and go to bed at 9:30 p.m., rain or shine, weekday or Sunday, and knowing the exact time was important to him. His most prized possession was the gold Elgin railroader's watch that he inherited from his brother Ben, a motorman on the Fort Worth–Dallas Interurban, who died after a collision with a horse-drawn wagon.

"A good watch will teach you the value of time," Ben said on his deathbed as he put the watch into Quill's hand.

Up to then Quill, like any farm-reared boy, had lived by suntime rather than by the hands of a clock. Ben's watch changed all that, except in one respect. He still preferred to shave of a morning by natural light. If the sun was not up when he got out of bed, he waited for it to rise before picking up the silver-handled straightedge razor that had belonged to his grandfather. It was Quill's second-most prized possession.

While waiting for the sun that first morning at Awahi, with Jane still sleeping, Quill unloaded the car. Despite Reverend Sandringham's warning about thieves, nothing had been touched. As the sun rose over Hawalanee and gradually lifted the pueblo out of the Sacred Mountain's shadow, Quill hauled in the last boxes from the car and prepared to shave.

Shaving was not something every man did every day, but it was almost as important as promptness to Quill, for whom a clean-shaven face signified position. A full beard or a well-trimmed Vandyke had once been acceptable for doctors and teachers and other professional men. The Great War and the spread of the safety razor, with its disposable blade, changed all that. Now most men of position shaved or were shaved daily. You seldom saw a bearded banker, doctor, lawyer, teacher, or successful merchant anymore, and never one with day-old whiskers darkening his chin. A schoolteacher who appeared in such a condition would instantly diminish his standing in Quill's eyes and, he believed, in all other eyes as well.

Preparing to use the razor, he unbuttoned the top two buttons of his shirt and folded the collar under to keep it from getting wet. Then he gave the razor, already sharpened after the previous day's shave, an extra swipe or two on his grandfather's old leather strop, which hung alongside the toothbrushes beside the sink. Bending his long frame to the mirror, he pulled the skin of his face taut with the fingers of one hand and began to take off his whiskers. As he shaved he thought about the meeting at which he had fallen from grace the previous summer at the Phoenix Indian Boarding School.

* * *

Quill and Jane joined other Indian Service employees from all over Arizona in a sweltering auditorium smelling of oiled floors and sweating bodies to hear a talk by a visitor from Washington, the commissioner of Indian affairs. Quill and Jane felt lucky to get seats by an open window, but even there they found no breath of air except that stirred by ceiling fans. Quill took off his suit coat, the only man in the room to do so.

The commissioner ordered the fans turned off. They were noisy and distracting, he said, and unnecessary.

"Being from D.C.," he said, as sweat trickled down his face and soaked his white linen suit, "I know what really hot August weather is. Heat without humidity, like you lucky folks have here, is as good as a mountain breeze to me. I find that if you don't think about being hot, you'll be quite comfortable."

As he droned through his speech, the commissioner reminded his perspiring listeners that more than a half-century earlier President Grant had replaced the U.S. government's long-standing Indian policy—he summarized it neatly if not quite accurately as "the only good Indian is a dead Indian"—with a more humane approach. Since Grant's time the official aim had been "to Christianize and civilize the Indian and to train him in the arts of peace," not kill him off.

The commissioner mentioned but brushed aside recent criticism of the policy, attributing it to "Young Turks and rabble-rousers." He named only John Collier of the American Indian Defense Association, and said, "Our task is unchanged. Today as in the past, we must strive to bring these savages to Jesus." He wiped his face with a sopping handkerchief and leaned over the podium, lowering his voice as though sharing a secret. "And by Christianize, President Grant did not mean Catholicize. Nor do I."

Throughout the room his listeners wiped brows along with the commissioner and nodded as he explained why he drew a distinction between Christianity and Roman Catholicism. Soon after the discovery of America, he said, Spanish priests imposed what he called "their foreign sect, neither fully Christian nor American" on the many Indian pueblos of what was now Arizona and New Mexico. And their successors were still at it. Franciscan priests even allowed Indians to mix their heathen rites with Christian observances. "We must continue to do all we can," the commissioner declared, "to help our brave Protestant missionaries do battle against Rome as well as paganism in these fertile vineyards of the Lord. Stand with them! See to it that they have all the weapons you can supply for their noble crusade against the Prince of Darkness."

His voice rising, he demanded rigorous enforcement of the long-standing rule forbidding children to speak their native tongues at government schools. Making little heathens use only English would wean them from their barbarous religions and allow Christ to claim their pagan souls. He concluded: "Whether yours is a day school or a boarding school, any time you hear a student speaking a savage tongue, whip that student publicly. The pain and humiliation will do as much as any sermon to bring the children to salvation and prepare them to live as civilized men and women."

Indian Service old-timers popped to their feet, applauding. One man, shouting, praised him for "keeping the faith." When the appreciative tumult died down, the commissioner thanked them for their support, but added, "I fear there is one among us who does not agree."

There was a wave of laughter, as though such a thing were unthinkable.

He pointed at Quill. "Would the coatless young gentleman in the third row by the window like to tell us why he found it necessary to shake his head at just about everything I have said?"

Quill stood up, putting on his coat. His left kneecap started jumping. Imperceptible to anyone else, its quivering felt to him as though his leg was about to buckle. It was something that happened every time he faced an argument.

"State your name, please," the commissioner said.

"Quill Thompson, sir. James McQuillian Thompson."

"And what is it that you so obviously disapprove of, Mr. James McQuillian Thompson?"

"Well, sir, it's not that I necessarily disapprove of 'Christianize and civilize'—"

"I'm glad to know that," the commissioner said, to more laughter.

"—but it seems to me that after all these years it's time to reexamine that policy. Lots of people are beginning to say that it's unconstitutional for the government to spend taxpayer money to help a church, regardless of denomination. And Indians resent our failure to recognize that they have religions and languages worthy of respect that are important to their history and culture. Besides, the policy just hasn't worked—Indians are worse off today than they were fifty years ago. They live in poverty and have few ways to make a living. Disease and epidemics are rampant. So maybe instead of trying to convert our pupils by punishing them for speaking their own language, we should let them be themselves. We should teach the children English and help them gain the other skills that will help them get along in the world as it is, not as we might like it to be. We can leave conversion—"

The commissioner cut him off before he could add "to the missionaries."

"Mr. Thompson, how long have you been in the Indian Service?"

"Three years, sir," Quill said.

"Just as I thought—a Young Turk. I suggest that you keep

your opinions to yourself until you have more experience to base them on. In other words, until you know what you're talking about. I also suggest that if you want to get ahead in the Indian Service you should not be so quick to accuse your superiors of breaking the law. Everything we do is for the good of the Indians and the nation—and I assure you, the Christianize and civilize policy is absolutely and perfectly legal and constitutional."

"I don't mean to question your judgment, sir. I just—"

"You already have, Mr. Thompson. Take your seat."

Quill sat down feeling like an unrepentant sinner at a camp meeting. He and Jane left the auditorium conspicuously alone.

* * *

Shaving on that first morning at Awahi, he saw a file of blanket-shrouded women trudging out of the pueblo to the river with water jars balanced on their heads. It was a sight that would greet him every morning at the break of day.

Chapter 5

They paused on the front porch of their house to look out over their domain. The stone barracks that had once housed cavalry troopers had been turned into the school's main entrance and central hall, with classrooms added along the sides. The additions had been built at different times over the years, each in a different style—an adobe wing here, a clapboard extension there. The old stable had been converted into the school kitchen and dining hall. The former bachelor officers' quarters had become a warehouse with bars on the windows. The magazine was now an icehouse. Frame buildings needing paint—separate bathhouses for boys and girls and bungalows for teachers and other white employees—encroached on the old parade ground. What remained of the quadrangle had become a basketball court, a small baseball diamond, and a playground with splintery teeter-totters, a slide, and a few swings swirling in the wind at the end of rusty chains.

"It's so forlorn," Jane said. She put her hand in Quill's.

They went first to the school. Steam radiators banged and chattered all through the building—whoever tended the boilers was already on the job—and the central hall and the classrooms opening off it were stifling. Quill tried to open a couple of windows, but found them nailed shut. The wooden floors were blackened with oil soaked up from the treated sawdust that janitors scattered to keep dust down as they swept. The building smelled like a garage filled with stripped-down Model T's waiting for repair.

Looking for a place to establish her clinic, Jane found a couple of adjoining small rooms that would get morning sun. One room had a sink and the other had doors opening to the outside as well as to the interior hall. Here, too, someone had nailed the outside door and the windows closed. The rooms were stuffed with old and apparently forgotten packing boxes, all empty. According to stenciled messages on the boxes, they had once contained items such as "Sweaters Wool Red Girls," "Overalls Bib Denim Boys All Sizes," "Shoes High Top Laced Girls All Sizes," and "Girls Full Length Black Stockings, Cotton."

While Jane tossed boxes out of her future clinic, Quill found the principal's office in a one-room adobe building next to but separate from the school. As he went to it he saw several Awahi men at work shoveling gravel into ruts in the muddy driveway leading into the compound. He called, "Good morning," and put up a hand in greeting. They ignored him and kept shoveling. An Awahi woman swept dried mud off the concrete sidewalk in front of the school. She, too, ignored him. No one else was around and no smoke rose from the chimneys of the teachers' cottages.

The office looked to Quill like a grander version of the one his Uncle Jim had once occupied as sheriff of Wilbarger County in West Texas. A wall-to-wall oak counter with a swinging gate divided the room into two parts. The area in front of the counter held two rows of pine benches. Beyond the barrier the furniture was oak—rolltop desk, filing cabinets, a cushioned desk chair on rollers, and two straight-backed chairs. In one corner a potbellied stove, a coal scuttle, and a spittoon stood on a tin-covered asbestos pad. A fire had been laid in the stove, ready for lighting. Tacked to the wall were a framed photograph of President Harding and a U.S. map printed on oilcloth, unframed and yellowed with age. The map was so old that Oklahoma, New Mexico, and Arizona were designated as territories.

The office was cold. Quill guessed that it had not been used since the departure of his predecessor. But despite the wind outside, there was no sand on the furniture or floor. Everything had been dusted, and the floor was clean and freshly oiled, perfuming the air with an acrid scent.

An Awahi man entered. Quill recognized him as one of the men he had seen filling ruts.

"Good morning," Quill said.

The man neither spoke nor looked at him as he put a match to the fire. The flame caught. He dropped the extinguished match in the coal scuttle and left while Quill was still trying to introduce himself. As Quill told Jane later, the man's message was clear: "You are the enemy."

In the rolltop desk Quill found a franked envelope (*"For Official Use Only. Penalty for Private Use $300."*) lying under an enormous ring of keys, each labeled. The envelope was addressed in a flowing Spencerian hand, "The New Principal, Whoever He May Be." Stuffed into it were a desk key and a fat sheaf of lined linen paper, each line filled with the beautifully formed letters of someone who prided himself on his penmanship. The document bore the heading "CONFIDENTIAL" and the salutation "Sir."

Before reading the missive, Quill flipped to the end. As he expected, it was from Joshua Wilman. The text proved to be a detailed complaint about the difficulty of the post and the unreliability of almost everyone that Quill and Jane would have to deal with at Awahi, the native population in particular.

"You will find the Awahis, even more than most Indians, to be sullen, immoral, uncooperative, much inclined to sloth and drunkenness, with a propensity for theft," Wilman wrote. "I have had to nail the classroom windows shut to guard against their depredations. For your own safety, I advise you to carry at all times the pistol Mr. Thornton has authorized for the personal use of the principal. You will find it loaded and locked in the lower desk drawer on the left. Carry it without fail if you have cause to go out at night (which, however, you should avoid doing)."

Quill unlocked the desk drawer and took out the pistol. It was a .45-caliber army revolver, fully loaded and holstered on an army cartridge belt. He emptied the chamber, put the gun and cartridge belt back in the drawer, relocked it, and turned back to the letter.

In it Wilman complained that many Awahis were subject to the long arm of Rome, in the person of the Franciscan priest, Father Aloyisus. Wilman attacked the priest as lazy and corrupt, adding that Reverend Sandringham of the Church of Jehovah's Sweet Light of Jesus Mission was attempting to find evidence—"so far, sadly, without success"—that Father Aloyisus was "misbehaving" with his altar boys.

In his long screed Wilman praised only the two Protestant missionaries at Awahi, the Reverends Sandringham and Housma, and Mrs. Wallis, whom he described as "my good right arm." Like Mr. Lasher, he commended her willingness to discipline female students. Again like Mr. Lasher, he dismissed the three young teachers on Quill's staff as nonentities but harmless. The same applied to the other two white employees—the school cook, Mrs. Stilton, and her husband, the "engineer" or maintenance man. Wilman condemned Mrs. Stilton as wasteful. He said she insisted on making her soups and stews thicker than Wilman thought necessary and dished out larger servings than required. Her husband he described as competent enough, but lazy.

Everyone else at Awahi, he denounced as an enemy of order, efficiency, and morality. He was especially hard on the trader, Sam Taylor. "He lives with an Awahi squaw and has many children by her, but I have never seen evidence of a marriage license. His children by her bear her name, not his, and his oldest son attends our school, as his mixed blood entitles him to do. Besides being immoral Taylor takes the part of the Indians in any dispute while cheating them of every dime he can. He keeps track of everything going on in the Pueblo, with the help of his squaw and her brother, Richard Lituka, a cripple who was once punished for witchcraft but now roams freely. He is a high school graduate, brought up in Michigan as a Christian, but now, sadly, a backslider. Watch out for him. He meddles in matters that do not concern him."

With Wilman's letter was a three-page list of equipment and supplies he claimed to be transferring to Quill's account, with instructions to "Sign and return this inventory to Mr. Lasher at Fort Frazier." Glancing over the inventory, Quill's eye fell on "20 Gross, Girls' Full Length Black Stockings, Cotton." Examining the list more closely, he found a couple of dozen such entries and realized that his predecessor was attempting to pass on to him the responsibility for accounting for the missing contents of all those boxes in Jane's clinic, some of them dating back twenty years and more. He put the list aside on the desktop, not to be signed until after he and Jane had taken their own inventory. When they did so, Wilman's inventory came down to a page and a half, which Quill signed and sent to Mr. Lasher. He never heard anything more about it.

* * *

Quill pulled out his watch. It was two hours past the traditional starting time of seven thirty, and he had seen no one but Awahi workers on the job. It was Saturday and classes would not be held, but government employees were expected to put in a half-day—although at remote posts like Awahi they were allowed two Saturdays off each month so that they could reach town while stores were open.

He decided to seek out his staff. Jane joined him in a tour of what in army days had been the quadrangle. There were five cottages, three with signs in front naming the occupants and two lacking signs and clearly unoccupied. Their first stop was at the Stilton cottage. No smoke rose from the chimney, and neither the cook nor the maintenance man answered Quill's knock.

"They must be out," Jane said.

"Probably gone to town."

The next cottage had three signs, each with a name. The front door opened as Quill and Jane started up the steps. Three young women, all about Jane's age and dressed alike in jodhpurs, heavy walking shoes, stocking caps, and short coats, came out and lined up on the porch. They smiled but looked wary.

"I'm Quill Thompson, the new principal, and this is my wife, Jane," Quill said.

Each young woman gave her name.

"Miss Ambler."

"Miss Tuttle."

"Miss Brewster."

They all looked alike to Quill, though blonde hair straggled from under the first stocking cap, brown from the second, and red from the third. Rows of gleaming white teeth. Cheeks rosy with rouge.

"We're just on our way out," Miss Ambler, the blonde, said.

"To the pueblo," said Miss Tuttle, the brunette.

"To see what's doing," said Miss Brewster, the redhead.

"Probably nothing," they chorused. And laughed.

"As usual," Miss Ambler added, giggling.

Quill and Jane stopped last at the cottage labeled "Wallis." A heavyset woman wearing a bright pink housedress opened the door a few inches, dabbing a napkin at the corner of her mouth. Yellowish hair, marcelled in deep waves, clung to her head like a helmet.

"Yes?"

"Mrs. Wallis?"

"Yes."

"I'm Quill Thompson. This is my wife, Jane."

Mrs. Wallis dabbed the other side of her mouth. "Yes?"

Quill felt his knee begin to jump. "I'm the new principal."

She made a sound in her throat. "Humph."

"May we come in?"

"I am having my breakfast."

"Please forgive the intrusion, Mrs. Wallis, but I had hoped to meet all the staff when they reported for work this morning."

"This is my town Saturday, Mr. Thomas. I would not be here now if the roads had been better." She slammed the door.

Jane said, "You can't let her get away with that. Mr. Thomas!"

"No," Quill said, "but I can try to find out what's sticking in her craw before I crack down."

"Good luck," she said. "If I were you, I'd go up there, open the door, and have it out with her right now."

"I can see you doing just that," he said, "but I'll bide my time."

His knee quivered.

Chapter 6

Blowing sand needled their skin as they picked their way hand in hand over the loose boards of the old bridge. Every now and again a strong gust made the bridge sway and groan underfoot. They could look down between the boards at the river trickling between ice-rimmed sandbars. A frayed rope sagging between stanchions served as a railing. Quill kept a hand on the rope as they crossed, and Jane kept a hand on him. On the far side, the pueblo side, they passed gardens made up of wafflelike squares just big enough to be irrigated with a single pot of water carried from the river on a woman's head. They saw only dried vines in the waffle gardens. But in spring, when snowmelt in the mountains fed the river a steady flow of water, the women's little squares would grow green with melon and squash vines, beans, peppers, and other vegetables. Men planted corn, a staple of the Awahi diet, in dry fields that might be many miles from both the pueblo and the river. Peach orchards clustered on the slopes below Hawalanee. Most farmers ran barefoot, stripped to breechclouts, to and from their fields and orchards each day, their clothes bundled on crude hoes over their shoulders. Only old men rode burros.

Beyond the gardens, captive eagles flapped their wings and screamed from evil-smelling pens built of brush, scraps of wood, and rusty chicken wire. Each spring Awahi boys aspiring to manhood climbed the rocky sides of Hawalanee to rob eagle nests just before young birds took flight. It was dangerous work—adult eagles protected their young with beak and claw and powerful wings. The nest-robbing boys often had to fight them off while clinging to sheer rock a hundred feet above the valley floor. Once seized, the fledglings were penned for life. Their feathers were pulled as needed to supply plumes for decorating ceremonial masks, costumes, and prayer sticks.

In corrals of logs, poles, brush, dried tumbleweeds, and rusted sheets of flattened tin cans, sheep and goats stood hoof-deep in manure. The goats, being inclined to climb out of the corrals and roam, were tethered as well as penned. Burros also were tethered. They bared yellow teeth and brayed insistently at passersby. Trash lay everywhere—horse and donkey droppings, small mounds of human feces, the frozen carcass of a rotting dog, half eaten by buzzards.

As they drew closer to the pueblo, they discovered that the clay plastered over the pueblo's adobe walls, which looked so white and pristine from a distance, was actually light brown. The clay had cracked and fallen away in great patches. Small sticks and bits of straw stuck out helter-skelter from the exposed adobes.

"The walls look like they have a bad case of ringworm," Jane said.

They strolled through the pueblo along passageways narrower than any automobile. Mere alleyways though they were, the streets were mostly free of trash, and the walls on either side had been freshly plastered. Scattered here and there small domed ovens, plastered like the houses with white clay, gave off whiffs of baking bread.

A village that from afar appeared uninhabited now teemed

with life. Quill and Jane nodded and spoke to the people they met. A few nodded back but none spoke. Men mostly strode past, ignoring them, while women averted their eyes and pressed against the wall, drawing shawls across their faces. Children were everywhere, many wearing the heavy wool sweaters issued to pupils at the government school, red for girls, dark gray for boys. They, too, drew against the walls. They could not keep from staring with owl-like black eyes opened wide, but none would admit to knowing English.

Jane pointed directly at a little girl in a red sweater and said, "I know you speak English. I see your sweater."

The girl shook her head, denying it.

"Told you so," Jane said, smiling.

They came across a broader passageway, wide enough for an automobile or small truck.

"Main Street," Quill said.

They followed the wider street as it meandered past and around the houses. After many turns, they found themselves at a central plaza, shielded from the wind by houses all around and warmed by the sun, which had finally emerged from the clouds. No ceremony was going on, but the plaza was crowded with people. Men leaned against the walls, chatting and smoking cigarettes they rolled from sacks of Bull Durham that passed from hand to hand. A white-haired potter sat with her back against a wall and her legs stretched out before her, forming a pot between her legs with coiled strings of wet clay. Young girls in school sweaters sat around her, their legs extended, too. They studied what she did and coiled their own clay strings into pots. Now and again the old potter would speak and gesture at a student, and the girls strained to hear, nodding.

Women swept in front of their doors with juniper-branch

brooms or grouped themselves along the walls, cradling babies and calling to toddlers. There were crying babies, laughter, and yapping dogs. Little boys chased one another across the open space. Larger ones tossed basketballs back and forth and raced from one point to another according to rules that Quill had no idea of. Little girls minded their younger brothers and sisters or rocked simple corncob dolls in their arms. One group in red school sweaters took turns hopping on one foot through squares scratched in the plaza floor.

"May I take a turn?" Jane asked the hopscotch girls.

A girl handed her a stone silently.

Jane tossed the stone, hopped through the squares, picked up the stone, and handed it back. The child took it without looking at her or making a sound and darted into a nearby doorway. And suddenly the plaza was all but empty of children.

"Well," Jane said. "I guess that wasn't such a good idea."

* * *

They came out of the pueblo on the far side, on a curve in the river. In a fenced enclosure they saw a ramshackle frame building, unpainted and scarcely larger than a six-hole privy. A steeple and a simple cross topped its flat roof. A neatly lettered wooden sign by the open gate said: "The Church of Jehovah's Sweet Light of Jesus Mission USA. Thomas Achilles Sandringham Jr. Pastor."

"Let's take a look," Quill said. "If Sandringham's at home we can thank him for the help he gave us last night."

Near the chapel was a well with a rope and bucket. Beyond it a crude shelter, too crude to merit so grand a word as "hut," looked like a trash pile. It was a tangle of crooked juniper logs of all lengths, carelessly chinked with bits of sagebrush and mud, with dried juniper branches, tumbleweeds, yucca, greasewood, and sagebrush. A shiny stovepipe thrust through a steeply sloped roof of small logs, flattened tin cans, tar paper, and canvas, covered with layers of brush. It was a windowless cave within a thicket.

"A firetrap," Jane said.

"Well, you can't say he's wasted money on his own comfort," Quill said.

Instead of Sandringham, they found a padlock on the hovel's door, a heavy homemade affair knocked together from old wood scraps and held up by hinges contrived from strips of old leather. As Quill pointed out, an intruder would have only to take a knife to the hinges and walk in.

Going back through the pueblo they ventured up a log ladder to the second level of houses and came upon a woman using a paddle to take freshly baked flatbread out of a domed oven. The woman ignored their greeting.

"I wish she'd offer us a slice," Jane said.

"No chance," Quill said.

They heard drumming and a rhythmic rattling beneath them and peered over the edge of the roof into a passageway that opened off the plaza, which again was bustling with life. A line of gourd-shaking dancers in brightly painted masks and intricately embroidered kilts filed past below. In the procession a little girl in a long white dress and a red sweater carried a pole topped by an image of the Virgin Mary painted on a board. Mud-smeared clowns wearing grotesque clay masks and little else cleared the way for the dancers and cavorted alongside them.

Reverend Sandringham raced into the plaza. His long black cloak and the tails of a voluminous frock coat flapped like wings around him. Golden hair, gray streaked, spilled down his shoulders from under a black bowler.

"Infidels, O INFIDELS, LISTEN to the WORD OF JEHO-

VAH," he thundered. "Turn away from your false gods. STRIKE THEM DOWN, ye savages! Ye SINNERS! Turn from the graven images of ROME! SPURN THE ANTICHRIST! SEEK SALVATION!"

Shouting, "SACRILEGE! O SACRILEGE!" he tried to pull the Virgin Mary from the little girl. The child screamed and wept but held onto the icon's pole.

Two mudheads seized Sandringham and pinned him against the plaza wall while the dancers made two circuits of the plaza. One mudhead reached up and clamped his hand over the missionary's mouth, muffling his cries. Other mudheads poked him in the ribs and grabbed at his genitals. One found a red rubber ball in the folds of the cloak and bounced it as he leaped and cavorted over the plaza. As soon as the dancers left the plaza the clowns released Sandringham and trotted off after them. The mudhead with the ball tossed it over his shoulder as he left.

The missionary shouted after them, "COME TO THE LORD! O COME TO THE LORD!"

Falling silent, he strolled around the plaza with the red rubber ball rolling up and down his arm and spinning around his hand. He seemed to pay no mind to what the ball was doing. Children stopped their play and followed him, keeping their distance.

A short, stout Catholic priest in a brown habit and broad-brimmed, flat-topped brown hat entered the plaza.

Sandringham stopped. The ball vanished. Neither Quill nor Jane saw where it went.

"SATAN INCARNATE! BACK! BACK, I say!"

He held his arms straight out in front of him. A Bible popped into his hands, held up like a barrier. Quill and Jane had no more idea where the Bible came from than where the ball had gone.

The priest seemed unperturbed by Sandringham's antics. He stopped and lifted his hat in greeting, with a slight bow.

Sandringham staggered backward on legs so long and stiff they might have been stilts. He waved the Bible before him with both hands.

"ROME!" he shouted. "WITCH! BE GONE! WITCH!"

The children scattered and fled at the first "witch."

Sandringham whirled around and around, spinning out of the plaza back the way he had come. His cloak flew about him and something different appeared in his hands on each circuit his body made—the Bible, his black bowler, a walking stick, or a ball. Each time a ball appeared it was a different color, now red, now blue, now green. He whirled around a corner and disappeared, still shouting.

"SATAN! ROME! WITCH!"

Quill and Jane went from the pueblo across the road to the trading post. It sprawled over several acres: store, residence, warehouses, barns, corrals, and a field where two cows and some horses grazed. The house was frame, newly painted in green-trimmed white, with a long screened porch across its front. The store was a pile of red stone, while the other buildings were adobes. As in the pueblo, the clay stucco had fallen away in places, showing the crude bricks. A red-and-black sign painted over the store's entrance in foot-high letters might once have read "AWAHI TRADING COMPANY" but was now so abraded by blowing sand that it said little more than "AW HI   DING COM." At a hitching rail in front, two burros dozed with noses almost touching the ground.

On a roofless stone porch, wooden benches defaced by generations of idle whittlers flanked a massive door of rough-hewn pine planks nailed diagonally on either side of vertical two-byeights. Barred windows were set deep in the thick walls above the benches. Quill pushed the door open and stumbled down two steps to the stone floor of a crowded bullpen.

A blast of wind came in with them. Coals flared in a flat-topped, potbellied stove resting on arched legs. A fresh whorl of smoke puffed from the stove. More smoke came from glowing cigarettes held between thumb and forefinger by Awahi men warming themselves at the stove and sitting on a benchlike ledge along one wall. Except for a few in bib overalls they wore velveteen tunics or denim shirts and shapeless pants of some heavy material that looked like canvas. Rolled kerchiefs held bobbed hair close to their skulls. Each man had a Pendleton blanket slung over his shoulder or resting on the bench beside him. Opposite the men, women sat with their blankets wrapped like shawls around their shoulders, though the murky room seemed hot. Children pressed against their skirts. Two of the women nursed infants.

Shelves loaded with goods lined one wall behind a broad counter. The shelves bore an astonishing mix of merchandise—baby bottles next to bib overalls, Pendleton blankets between cans of Van Camp's pork and beans and Vienna sausages, fifty-pound sacks of Pillsbury flour beneath high-crowned Stetson hats and high-topped women's shoes, bolts of bright calico and velveteen beside boxes of Carter's Little Liver Pills and Lydia Pinkham's female remedies. Saddles, scythes, plows, washtubs, cooking pots, and even a small cooking stove dangled from the ceiling. A gasoline lantern hissed amid the clutter, sending a harsh white light through the swirling smoke, along with eerie shadows of the objects hanging around it.

On the counter beside a National Cash Register a large green glass jar held striped candies and brightly colored jawbreakers. Next to it a roll of brown butcher paper rested in a shiny brass dispenser. A coarse brown string came up through a hole in the counter, unwinding as needed from an unseen cone under the counter. On the shelf behind the register a hand-cranked mill stood ready to grind the beans spilling from a half-empty burlap sack marked "Arbuckle's Coffee" that slumped on the floor.

A woman at the counter had a No. 10 can of stewed tomatoes and two cans of condensed milk on the counter in front of her. She was pointing at something on the shelf. As they entered she froze, finger in midair, her mouth filled with unspoken words.

The trader looked up, pushing a sweat-stained Stetson to the back of his head. He was a wiry little man with weather-browned skin and tobacco-stained teeth. He wore faded Levis and a denim work shirt. One eye wandered aimlessly around its socket. The other focused on Quill and Jane.

"Come on in," the trader said, in a high-pitched nasal voice. "Be with you soon's I finish with this here customer."

Quill turned to the men at the stove.

"I'm Quill Thompson," he said, sticking out his hand. "The new principal. I'm glad to see you."

Two men stared blankly at him and turned away without taking his hand. Two others touched his hand, though neither said a word. Nor did they look at him. Smiling and nodding, Quill turned to the men on the benches, with about the same result, while Jane went over to the women. They looked at her with what she felt were appraising eyes and drew their shawls more closely around themselves. None returned her greeting.

The trader finished with his customer. "I'm Sam Taylor," he said.

Words streamed out of him like beans from the Arbuckle's

sack. He spoke like a man who has a lot to say and no one to say it to most of the time. "Folks been telling me you was sight-seeing in the pueblo on your way here. Ain't every day we get a new anybody here at Awahi, least often a new principal and his wife, and folks is naturally interested. You'll find there ain't nothing you do here that ain't going to be talked about. You'll get used to it. Ain't so much that we're a nosy bunch, though we're that, too, but folks just naturally keep track day to day, minute to minute of who's doing what, not to mention why and to who. Small town, you know. Not much to do but watch each other and not approve of most of what we see. So welcome to our fair city. What can I do for you?"

Jane waved postcards at him. "Where can I mail these?"

"Right here," Taylor said. He pointed to a slot in the counter. "This here's a official United States Post Office. It'll go out in the next mail."

"When will that be?"

"God knows. Depends on when somebody goes to town or a truck comes here. Don't happen every day."

When the trader learned that Jane was a nurse and would be setting up a clinic, he said, "Now ain't that something? A nurse! First time in I don't know how long since we seen a living, breathing medical person here at Awahi. And then they just come in and look around a day or two like tourists before they skedaddle back to town. Don't be too surprised if folks is slow to warm up to having you look down their throats. They got their own remedies they been using for centuries maybe and is slow to change their ways. Besides, they don't cotton much to strangers, especially whites. Strangers has been bad news around here since the Spaniards marched in way back ago."

"I hope I can do some good," Jane said.

"Well, how you act, that's what'll make a difference, and you started off good, shaking hands all around like you done just now. Don't many whites bother to shake hands with Indians in these parts. Wilman sure as hell never done nothing like that. What you done, a little thing like that, it'll help. And like when you took your turn at hopscotch over at the plaza like I hear you done, you made friends with a lot more little girls than was in the plaza at the time. Ain't many folks ain't heard about that by now."

He took a few minutes to wait on another customer and then returned to the subject.

"My wife's expecting again," he said. "I'll get her to come see you. That'll maybe help. She's Awahi—hell, I been here so long, almost since the turn of the century, I'm more Awahi than not. Her going to you could maybe ease the way for others to do the same. Besides, it'll make me feel better and can't do her no harm."

"I'll make sure of that," Jane said, smiling. "I look forward to meeting her."

"Wish she was here right now," the trader said, "but she's over in the pueblo visiting her sisters."

"We walked through the pueblo a while ago and stumbled on Reverend Sandringham's chapel," Quill said.

"Heard you did," Taylor said, tapping tobacco into a cigarette paper, "'Round here we just call him the missionary."

He paused while he got the cigarette rolled and lighted. "Heard you seen him at the plaza, too."

"Yes. It was—it was strange," Jane said.

"Yeah, strange," Taylor said. "I was the one brought him here, twenty years or more ago, and I been regretting it ever since."

Chapter 7

Sam Taylor told the story. He was just a youngster at the time and learning the Indian trading business from old John Purvis, who then owned the Awahi post. Purvis sent him to Gallup to sell a wagonload of wool, hides, and a few fine examples of Awahi silver-and-turquoise jewelry. He was supposed to spend the proceeds on merchandise for the trading post. But by the time he'd sold the hides and jewelry it was late in the day, and he found himself with a night to kill and money in his pocket, his own as well as Purvis's. He went on a bender, a first for him. After sampling the wares at several of the town's twelve saloons and four—the trader hesitated, with a glance at Jane— "houses of entertainment," he found himself alone at a crowded Railroad Avenue establishment incongruously called Mrs. Conner's Soda Parlor.

Feeling an urgent need for further female companionship, he looked around him. The only woman he could see sat at a large round table with a half-dozen big-bellied, florid-faced, loud-voiced men, one of whom had an arm draped over her shoulders. She was young, redheaded, with a tinkling laugh that, though not loud, rang cheerily over the roar of male voices. Sam thought she was beautiful—too beautiful to be wasted on that bunch of geezers, every one of them old enough to be her father.

None too directly—despite his best efforts to steer a steady course, his legs kept zigging and zagging, not always on command—Sam crossed from the bar to face the pretty redhead across the big round table. Pushing his way between two of the old-timers, he leaned across the table, holding it down with his outspread hands to stop its spinning, and smiled at her.

"Hey, girlie," he remembered saying, "whatcha doing with the old folks? Lemme buy you a drink and le's have some fun."

The next thing Sam remembered he was in a muddy ditch between the board sidewalk in front of Mrs. Conner's establishment and the rutted dirt street, where a gutter would have been, had Gallup been provided with such an amenity at the time. As from a great distance, he heard a deep, resonant voice with a cornpone Southern accent, which Sam imitated, "Lawd! Lawd, have muhcy on this PO' MISGUIDED YOUNG'UN! Let him FIND THE WAY, Lawd!"

"Here, now," Sam tried to say. All that came out was a groan.

"Ah! You're coming 'round."

Sam managed to open an eye. In the dim light of the not-quite-risen sun he made out a man about his own age bending over him, fanning him with a black bowler hat. Except for a white shirt and celluloid collar, the man was dressed all in black—shiny shoes, peg trousers, and a long frock coat, both coat and trousers cut with exceptional fullness. Even in his blurry state, Sam thought he had never seen a handsomer man. He had smooth skin, chiseled features, a dimple in one cheek, a cleft in the chin, blond hair pomaded straight back from a high forehead, the hair long enough to fall to his shoulders, and blue green eyes burning within a fringe of what looked to be double rows of lashes.

"Where am I?" Sam asked.

The man in black helped him sit up. "In the gutter, I fear, my young friend sunk in sin (O! SUNK!) and feeble in health—bloodied (O! BLOODIED!) but not yet, the GOOD LORD PERMITTING and you repenting, NOT YET at the END!"

Each time the man shouted a word, Sam jumped. It was like having an ax blade dropped on his head.

"Listen," he pleaded. "I feel god-awful and I can't see real good. I need a beer and shot."

"What you need is a good long drink—"

"Sounds good!"

"—of the WORD OF GOD and a SINCERE PRAYER for forgiveness. REPENT! Young man, REPENT! And in the meantime, you need a doctor."

"I'm fine."

"But your eye ain't. It's hanging halfway down your cheek. Somebody's got to shove it back in the socket and I ain't the one to do it. I don't know how."

A westbound coal train whistled into town along the Santa Fe tracks on the other side of Railroad Avenue. Again the ax blade smashed Sam's skull.

"Whyn't he shut up?" Sam demanded.

"He'll be stopping to take on water. That'll cut him off."

As the coal train slowed, an eastbound passenger express hurtled past on another track, going the other way. The two trains shrieked and chortled like braying donkeys through what seemed to Sam a lengthy conversation.

He groaned, turned his head. Vomited.

The man who would become known as the missionary handed him a red kerchief. Sam wiped his lips and then examined the kerchief.

"That's mine," he said.

"About all they left, looks like," the missionary said. "Turned your pockets out."

Sam felt his pockets frantically. Mr. Purvis's money was gone, along with the remnants of Sam's own stake—even his lucky dollar, minted in 1883, the year of his birth. It had a copper loop soldered on the back, indicating that it had once been displayed on a Navajo medicine man's necklace. He had found it on the steps of the Awahi Trading Post the day he went there to ask Mr. Purvis for a job. No one had ever appeared to claim it, and since he got the job, he regarded it as his lucky dollar. He would not have parted with it for anything.

"Somebody's stole my money. Got my '83 lucky dollar and the hide money, too! Mr. Purvis'll kill me. Who stole my money?"

"One of those ranchers, no doubt, before I could stop them."

Sam threw up again, leaning on an elbow, sobbing uncontrollably.

"Ah, SIN! It is not the money you should worry about, young man. It is your SOUL. Think of your IMMORTAL SOUL! You have lain with EVIL women. You have FORNICATED. You have sinned grievously. GRIEVOUSLY! You have set your feet on the PATH TO HELL! Turn back, O my friend, TURN BACK! FIRE and DAMNATION await you. FIRE! DAMNATION! You have DRUNK the Devil's brew. Repent, young man, REPENT!"

Worrying more about Mr. Purvis than hell, Sam declared, "I do. I'll never take another drink."

The missionary helped him to his feet. "BLESS YOU, Brother! You have WHIPPED the DEMON RUM! You have taken the FIRST STEP TO SALVATION. And now we must find a doctor to take care of that eye."

At an office above a hardware store on Coal Avenue, the Gallup street where respectable people shopped, they had to wait a couple of hours for the doctor to show up. When he appeared, unshaven and with shaking hands, he wasted no time in seizing Sam's eye where it dangled on his cheek and thrusting it back into place. Tightly binding Sam's head with bandages and smearing iodine on sundry cuts and abrasions, the doctor charged a dollar. The missionary, invoking the Lord's name along with a mention of the Good Samaritan, offered fifty cents. The doctor accepted seventy-five, which the missionary paid grudgingly. He told Sam, "You can repay me when you're on your feet again."

Supported by the missionary, Sam tottered back to the edge of town, where he had left his four-mule team and wagon. The two Awahi men who had accompanied him to Gallup had a campfire going beside the wagon, with a pot of coffee boiling and a No. 10 can of baked beans warming in the coals.

Forcing beans into a reluctant stomach, Sam heard the missionary begin to pray, starting with grateful thanks for the bountiful food they were about to partake of and moving on to further thanks for the miracle of the missionary's having been present when Sam foolishly approached Dan Wagner's innocent daughter with sinful intent, arousing the righteous wrath of her father, whom the Lord in His wisdom, assisted by Wagner's formidable political connections, had made the richest rancher between Albuquerque and Phoenix, with grazing rights over half the vast Navajo reservation.

Sam had no independent recollection of what happened after he leaned across the spinning table to offer a drink to what he thought was a pretty little whore. He learned a good deal about the ensuing brouhaha as the missionary told the Lord how he had been strolling along Railroad Avenue, silently praying for the immortal souls of the sinners gamboling within its dives when he passed in front of Mrs. Connor's Soda Parlor and heard angry yells, blasphemous threats, cries of pain, and the heart-rending screams of a woman beset. Rushing inside, he saw the rancher strike Sam across the face and body with the butt of not one but two six-guns, while the girl wept and the father's companions added fists and sharp-pointed boots to the one-sided fray.

Viewing what threatened to turn into a massacre, the missionary held up his Bible, which as always was close at hand, and shouted, "STOP! In the name of the Lord, STOP!"

And they stopped.

"A MIRACLE!" For which the missionary gave THANKS TO THE LORD, on his behalf as well as Sam's.

Having prayed, the missionary sat on a rock facing Sam and tucked into a plate of beans and bread. He ate slowly, fastidiously, not allowing his hunk of bread to soak up bean juice but keeping it dry at one side and nibbling at it from time to time with pinkie lifted, as though he were at a persnickety aunt's tea table. Between mouthfuls he offered a few fragments of information about himself. He gave his name as Thomas Achilles Sandringham Jr. and his age as twenty-four. He was, he said, a traveling preacher from Montgomery County, Alabama, and he was seeking the place the Lord had called him to.

"What place is that?" Sam asked.

"I'll know when I get there," the young man said. He added little more information about himself, and even those few crumbs were unrevealing—that he liked beans almost as well as beef and that while he preferred his coffee with real cream, he had no objection to condensed milk from a can when, as now, circumstances (and the Lord) so arranged it.

As he filled with beans he began to ask questions about Awahi. About its people. About Sam and Mr. Purvis. He nodded his head from time to time, but otherwise did little to indicate more interest in one thing than in another. He finished spooning up his beans and savored the last of the chunks of salt pork with which they had been well larded. At last he dipped his bread into the remaining bean juice and wiped his plate with his bread just as any man would, pinky down.

"I thank you, Brother, for your hospitality."

"You saved my life," Sam reminded him.

"Not I, Brother. The Lord. The LORD it was who reached DOWN to you and SAVED you from PAYING THE PRICE OF FOLLY."

Sam groaned. "Not the full price. I still got to face Mr. Purvis. What's he going to say? I got fifty dollars for them hides and jewelry and don't have a dime to show for it. And he needs the supplies I'm supposed to buy."

"Perhaps a bank loan?" the missionary suggested. "I saw a fine-looking establishment in a stone building with columns on Coal Avenue, the McKinley County State Bank."

Sam was young but not naïve in financial matters. "Not a chance. Don't nobody here know me."

He groaned and contemplated throwing up again, beans and all.

"I have a suggestion," the missionary said. He held out his hand as though to shake Sam's. A dollar bill popped into view between his index and second fingers. While Sam watched, a silver dollar appeared between the missionary's second and third fingers, and, almost simultaneously, a golden eagle showed up between the third and last fingers, while another banknote—Sam could not make out the denomination—waved momentarily at the tip of his thumb before falling into the palm of his hand, which suddenly filled with coins.

Without saying a word, the missionary transferred the lode to Sam's hand. He pulled Sam's ear. Money poured out. He stacked that in Sam's hand, too.

"How did you do that?"

"The Lord giveth and the Lord taketh away, but He looketh after His own," the missionary said. "The Lord has spoken. Awahi is where He means me to go. My suggestion is this. By the Lord's gracious intervention I am well provided with funds at the present time. Let me replace your losses. You can pay for Mr. Purvis's trading post supplies and we will return together to Awahi. I shall establish my mission there and each month, you will give me half your wages until the debt is repaid. Without interest, Brother, so long as you keep your pledge to turn your back on DEMON RUM."

Sam wept with gratitude and shook hands on the deal.

That, the trader said, was how the missionary came to Awahi. "And I ain't had a drink since."

* * *

As Quill and Jane left, the trader pushed open the swinging gate at the end of the counter and joined them on the stone porch. Though he spent his days behind a counter, his mud- and manure-encrusted boots looked as though he had been toiling in fields and corrals. After the dimness of the bullpen the sun seemed brighter than ever, but no warmer. As usual, the wind was strong and biting. Jane pulled her Hudson's Bay coat close about her.

"Does the wind ever stop?" she asked.

"Not to speak of," Taylor said. "It comes down out of them mountains like a runaway train out of a tunnel. And when it does stop, believe it or not, it always brings bad luck. That's what us Awahis say, anyway."

"We're used to wind," Quill said. "We're from West Texas."

A one-cylinder Excelsior motorcycle, an old prewar model, putt-putted up the road and stopped in front of the post. The rider, an Awahi man, lifted green glass goggles onto his forehead before dismounting. He had gray-streaked black hair, squared off and bobbed below the ears. A rolled red bandanna wreathed his head. He wore dungarees, a faded blue shirt, and a mackinaw out at the elbows. The toes of his muddy boots were worn through and the soles were loose, bound to the uppers only by strips cut from old inner tubes. Hunch-shouldered and bent, he lurched off the Excelsior and lifted a cardboard carton stenciled "Gallup Mercantile Co." from a small wooden platform built where a second seat had once been. Throwing himself stiff-leggedly from side to side like a man walking on stilts, he carried the box up the steps.

"This here's my wife's brother, Richard Lituka," the trader said. "Richard helps me around the place. Even keeps my books."

Richard nodded and made a sound like "arrgh" deep in his throat as he stumbled past them into the post carrying the Gallup Mercantile carton.

"Richard don't say much," Taylor said. "His voice box got crushed a long time ago. Same time the rest of him got so twisted and hurt."

"He keeps your books?" Quill asked.

"Funny, ain't it? Richard don't look it, but he's got a lot more education than me. Hell, I never made it past the fourth grade. But Richard grew up in Michigan. He's got him a high school diploma and knows all about accounting. He reads a whole book in less time than it takes me to get through the Gallup *Independent.* Gets a box of books from the State Library in Santa Fe every few weeks. Reads every one, all the way through. Don't know how he does it."

"What happened to him?" Jane asked.

"Ah!" Taylor said. "It's a long story, all about witchcraft and a maybe foolish young man—something like me at Mrs. Connor's Soda Parlor. Too long a story to go into standing out here in this here wind. I'll tell you about Richard next time you're by. It's a story will tell you a lot about us folks at Awahi, what we worry about and what we do, which ain't always the smartest thing in the book."

Chapter 8

On Monday morning the sun was bright, but ice sparkled on the river, and the warmest coat could not fend off the cold wind. Quill held a short meeting in his office. He told the teachers to follow their usual routine because he wanted to observe for a while before making any changes. He invited suggestions and comments, but the younger teachers did not seem interested, which indicated to Quill that they were so used to being ignored they didn't think it worthwhile to express their views. Mrs. Wallis was quick to speak up. She said she presumed he knew that she had acted as deputy principal under Mr. Wilman and as acting principal in his absence.

"I suggest you continue that arrangement," she said. "Mr. Wilman found it advantageous. It gave him time to deal with the Indians, while I administered the school."

"We'll see," Quill said. His knee quivered.

She ignored his equivocation. "We start each day with a flag ceremony," she said. "We think it's important to remind them that they are now Americans."

A whistle hung on a chain around her neck. She moved as though to take it off. "Perhaps you'd prefer to take charge of the ceremony this morning?"

"I think not," Quill said.

• • •

Children in red and gray sweaters poured across the bridge from the pueblo, chattering and laughing. Watching from the school steps Quill noted that laughter stopped when the children reached the schoolyard. Boys continued to elbow, shove, and kick, but did so quietly, keeping a lookout for Mrs. Wallis. Little girls whispered to one another and giggled softly now and again, but not when Mrs. Wallis was near.

The flag raising went off with military precision. Mrs. Wallis blew her whistle. Teachers took their places beside her on the playground. Children lined up in front of them class by class, girls in one shivering row, boys in another. Mrs. Wallis took the roll of fourth, fifth, and sixth graders and announced the number in attendance. The other teachers did the same with their classes: Miss Ambler for the first grade, Miss Tuttle for the second, and Miss Brewster for the third. As they called out the totals of those present in each class and the names of those who were tardy or absent, Mrs. Wallis recorded the names and figures in an account book.

One of her sixth-grade boys dashed up just as she was closing the book.

"You are late, Nathan," she said. "See me after the ceremony." She entered his name on the tardy list. He fell into line glumly, as though already feeling the birch.

With everyone in her class lined up, she moved to the school steps, where she blew one short blast on her whistle. An Awahi man emerged from a door at the side of the steps, bearing a folded flag in his upturned hands. Quill recognized him as the man who had lit the fire in his office on Saturday morning. He still did not know his name. The man marched out to a flagpole at the edge of the school grounds next to the road, midway between the principal's house and the school.

Mrs. Wallis blew her whistle again. The students pivoted to face the pole. The Awahi man raised the flag.

Another whistle blast. A sixth-grade boy stepped to the base of the flagpole and faced the assembled children.

Whistle. The students placed hands over hearts—Quill hastily followed suit—and with the sixth grader leading them they shouted out the Pledge of Allegiance, not quite in unison but close enough. The flag flapped in the wind.

Whistle. The children wheeled to face the school and Mrs. Wallis.

A final whistle.

"Go to your classes," Mrs. Wallis said.

The students marched in class by class, first graders in the lead.

Quill went to Mrs. Wallis.

"What's the name of the man who raised the flag?" he asked.

"I've no idea. He's just a handyman."

* * *

Quill allowed time for the children to settle down after the flag ceremony before he made a tour of the classrooms, starting with Miss Ambler's first grade. He paused in the hallway before rapping on her door.

"Chair," he heard Miss Ambler say. "Chair. This is a chair."

A child said something in Awahi, along with, "Chair. This is a chair."

A chorus then repeated, raggedly, "Chair. This a chair."

Miss Ambler said, "That's very good, children, very good."

There was an outburst of laughter and Awahi, with the word "chair" mixed in.

Quill pushed the door open. The children, girls on one side of a center aisle, boys on the other side, lost their smiles and fell silent. Miss Ambler froze, holding a child's small red chair over her blonde head.

"I'm so sorry, Mr. Thompson," she said, lowering the chair. "I didn't know you were there. That is—I mean—"

"I'm sorry to interrupt. I just wanted to introduce myself to the children, if you don't mind."

"Please do," Miss Ambler said, "though I'm afraid not many will understand."

"I'll keep it simple," Quill said, "and I'm sure the ones who do understand will tell the others what I've said after I leave."

He smiled at her and turned to the children. Expectant faces stared from desks in crowded rows. Some of the students at the end of the rows were too large for their desks and sat sideways, feet in the aisles—Awahi parents often kept their children out of school until they were eight or even ten years old. The walls of the room were festooned with bright paper chains and drawings, many of them of kachinas in full regalia. A radiator banged along one wall.

Speaking slowly, Quill said, "My name is Mr. Thompson. I have come to Awahi to live among you and to help you learn. I don't know your names yet, but I am glad to see you. You have a very pretty room and a very good teacher. I will come to see you again soon."

He turned to Miss Ambler. "Thanks for letting me speak to your class. I should have told you that I might be dropping by. Now carry on, just as you were."

As he went down the hall to the next room he heard a subversive clamor of Awahi behind him and Miss Ambler saying, panic in her voice, "Children, children, please be quiet. Please speak English."

* * *

His visits to Miss Tuttle's room and Miss Brewster's went about the same. Finally he knocked, leg twitching, at the door of Mrs. Wallis's classroom, where she taught the three upper grades in the mornings, but only the fourth grade after the daily hot lunch. In the afternoons Mr. and Mrs. Stilton gave the fifth and sixth graders what Mr. Lasher at Fort Frazier had called "practical instruction" by assigning them unpaid but essential jobs around the school. The girls washed dishes, scrubbed floors, and laundered the towels supplied to pupils for their weekly shower. Boys oiled and swept floors, washed windows, and occasionally dug ditches or learned how to tighten a leaking pipe. Quill saw little useful instruction in any of the chores. Awahi houses did not have wooden floors to scrub or oil. Nor did they have plumbing to repair.

All was silent within as he rapped on Mrs. Wallis's door. Rather than go on in, as he had at the other rooms, he waited.

Mrs. Wallis poked her head around the door. Over her head he caught a glimpse of stony-faced children sitting up straight, arms stretched out on top of their desks. Heads did not turn, but eyes aimed at the door.

"Yes?"

"May I come in? I'd like to say a few words to the children, introduce myself."

"That will not be necessary."

"I think it is," Quill said. He pushed the door open.

"Rise, children! Stand up for Mr. Thompson."

She had a switch in her hand. In the front of the room, the tardy sixth grader was bent over her desk with his elbows resting on it.

"Nathan, go to your seat. I shall deal with you later."

"Perhaps we should step out in the hall," Quill said.

"You have no business barging in," she said, but she followed him out of the room.

"Mrs. Wallis, I am the principal, and corporal punishment is not to be administered except with my permission, which I have not given in this or any other case."

"That boy is incorrigible. He was late to school this morning, as you must have seen, and just now he spoke Awahi to me in front of the entire class, out loud and in a disrespectful tone."

"What did he say?"

"How would I know? It was in Awahi."

"Hereafter, Mrs. Wallis, you are to get my permission before whipping any pupil for any reason."

"That is a mistake, Mr. Thompson. A serious mistake."

"Perhaps," Quill said. His knee quivered. "But that is the way it is going to be."

"You should wait until you know more about these Awahis before taking a drastic step like this. Whipping is the only way to get anything into their thick skulls."

"I know children, Mrs. Wallis, and I have never known a child to be improved by a beating."

She refused to be diverted. "How am I supposed to maintain discipline at this school when you fail to enforce the most basic precept of the Indian Service?"

"Which precept is that, Mrs. Wallis?"

"You know very well what I mean. That the pupils must speak English and only English while in school. I observed several instances this morning when you might have taken action and did not."

"I see. But I don't know what you mean about your maintaining discipline at this school. I am the person charged with that duty."

"A duty you show no intention of carrying out. Someone has to do it."

"Mrs. Wallis, you are coming very close to insubordination."

"Nonsense. You are no longer in the army, Mr. Thompson, and I refuse to be treated as though you're a colonel and I'm a private."

Quill laughed. "I don't think my army service affects my behavior in any way. I was a buck private and not that for very long."

"Just long enough, I suppose, to claim the veteran's preference points that let you take a job that should have gone to people with better qualifications and longer experience than you."

"Is that the problem, Mrs. Wallis? You feel you should be in this job?"

"There's no doubt about it. Mr. Wilman as much as promised it to me."

"Was it his to promise?"

"I believe it was, and I understand Mr. Lasher was prepared to back me. Then you came along with your veteran's points and influential friends and spineless ways."

"Influential friends?"

"Don't think we don't all know that it was your special friend, the commissioner of Indian affairs, who overruled the people in the field, the people who know something about Indian education. Instead of following their recommendations, he appointed an ignorant upstart as principal."

"Mrs. Wallis, that is quite enough. You may go back to your class now."

"Humph," she said.

He did not try to correct her misapprehension about his standing in Washington. He thought influential friends, even nonexistent ones, might come in handy.

Chapter 9

Richard Lituka's one-lung Excelsior putt-putted through the school's rusty iron gate. A middle-aged Awahi woman rode on the platform behind him, facing backward, legs outthrust. Richard pulled up in front of Jane's clinic-to-be. His passenger marched to the door ahead of him. She was short and sturdy, with a rectangular shape that was all straight lines and sharp angles. Black hair squared off below her ears and just above her eyes framed her round face like a proscenium.

Under the ubiquitous Pendleton blanket worn as a shawl, her costume was a mix of Pueblo and what at Awahi was called "American" styles. Over a pink and blue calico housedress she wore a short black tunic draped over one shoulder and girded by a colorful sash, the fringes of which dangled at her side. Both tunic and sash were of tightly woven hand-spun wool, brightly embroidered. Leggings of wide strips of white cloth showed above well-worn black high-tops, factory made, like those offered for sale at the trading post.

Jane was on her knees scrubbing the floor with disinfectant when the couple walked in without knocking, as was the Awahi custom. She rocked back on her heels. "Hello, Mr. Lituka. May I help you?"

She could not make out what he replied. After repeating it a time or two he turned to the woman beside him.

Speaking in a soft clear monotone, she said, "Richard want

me to say, I am his sister, Lina Lituka. I am wife of Ninsulka, the Rain Priest of the North."

"I'm glad to meet you, Mrs. Ninsulka."

"No. I keep my name. That is what women do at Awahi. I am Mrs. Lituka."

Richard spoke again.

"Richard, he say he want to work for you. He say he is strong. He know English, how to read and write. He know how to scrub, too. He don't talk so good, but you need interpreter for Awahi anyway. I work for you and interpret Richard like I interpret Awahi. I interpret for Mr. Thompson, too, if he want."

"Doesn't Richard work for Mr. Taylor at the trading post?"

"Sam say it all right for Richard to work for you some of time and him rest of time. I work for you and Mr. Thompson all time."

Jane asked a few questions. She established that Lina Lituka had learned her English at the Catholic school, which she had attended for six years, going through all four of the grades it offered at the time. She seemed to have a good vocabulary, but little use for articles, which she used erratically if at all, or other fine points of grammar. Still, Jane felt she spoke well and confidently. Lina had held various jobs under Mr. Wilman and his predecessors—bathhouse attendant, laundry woman, and most recently, girls' matron. She had never been paid as an interpreter but had often served in that capacity for Awahis who met with Mr. Wilman. She explained that Mr. Wilman had refused to hire interpreters, but required anyone wishing to speak to him to use English or bring an interpreter to the meeting. She was not presently employed, she said, having been fired as girls' matron by Mr. Wilman.

"Why did he fire you, Mrs. Lituka?"

She shrugged. "I don't like missionary."

"But why would Mr. Wilman fire you for not liking the missionary?"

"Mr. Wilman say it don't matter I like somebody or not. He say it not my business what the missionary say or do."

"The missionary said something or did something you didn't like?"

"He order everybody around. He talk mean. He yell at people. He call us names. He make the girls cry."

"Let me think about the permanent jobs," Jane said. "But I could certainly use both of you right now. When can you start?"

Lina draped her shawl over a chair. "Now," she said.

* * *

Sam Taylor confirmed that it was all right with him if Richard wanted to work for Jane.

"Richard, he's just what you need," he told her. Still talking he pulled a bag of Bull Durham from a shirt pocket, rolled a cigarette, and struck a match on the sole of his shoe. "He's smart and he's interested in sanitation, things like that—hell, that's part of what got him in trouble and left him in the shape he's in. You won't need him full-time, at least not at first, and he'll still have time for my books."

As for Lina, Taylor added, she would be a good choice as interpreter. "I knew her well," he said. "She speaks English better than anyone else in the village outside of my wife—better than I can speak Awahi, even after all the years I been here." Just as important, she was from one of the most respected Awahi families, at the top of the Awahi social ladder, and a leader among Awahi women.

"That matters more'n you might expect," the trader explained. "It's the women run the families and have a big say in most everything that matters. Oh, they let the men deal with the gods and the U.S. government—what you might call foreign affairs—but it's the women that owns the property and sees to it that the kids is took care of. And it don't hurt that she's married to Ninsulka, Rain Priest of the North. He's top dog on the religion side and a powerful man. Him and the governor pretty much run the place or leastways think they do. Lina knows everything that goes on and where the bodies is buried."

"Why did Mr. Wilman fire her?" Jane asked. "Mrs. Lituka said it was something about the missionary."

"Not real sure. What Lina thinks Lina says right out, and she don't watch out for nobody's toes. Wilman used to say he couldn't stand a uppity Indian."

"And that's what got Lina fired?"

"Who's to say? Wilman and the missionary was big buddies."

"You said Richard's interest in things like sanitation got him in the shape he's in," Quill said. "Tell us about that, if you've got the time."

"I got nothing but time," the trader said. The cigarette seemed glued to his lip and wobbled up and down as he talked. Ashes formed and dropped unnoticed. "To know about Richard," he said, "you got to know about witches at Awahi."

"You believe a witch did that to Richard?"

"No, I ain't Awahi enough for that. I don't believe in witches, no more than you. But you go out and ask the first Awahi you see, you believe in witches? He'll think you're crazy. Believe? Ain't no Awahi don't believe in witches. A long time ago folks decided Richard was a witch. When the wind died, he wound up like he is now, just about wrecked."

"What did the wind have to do with it?"

"A witch, you see, he gets his power from the wind—Awahi witches is most always a he. When the wind dies he loses his power and the folks who think he's a witch goes after him. And that's what happened to Richard."

The trader dropped his cigarette butt on the stone floor, not bothering to step on it, and again took out his sack of Bull Durham.

"It started a long time ago, years before I ever heard of Awahi," he said, lighting up. "Lina and Richard was little kids who hadn't seen more than a half-dozen whites in their whole lives, if that, and my wife, who's their little sister, wasn't even born, when folks here had a long run of bad luck. Drought, poor crops, healthy young women dying in childbirth, a rattlesnake slipping into a house and biting a baby—that sort of thing."

One winter day, a group of Awahi women went to the river to get water. As they returned with full pots balanced on their heads, enemy raiders seized the women and carried them away. The pots of the captured women fell to the ground and shattered—in Awahi eyes a sure sign of a witch at work. No one knew who the raiders were. Navajos? Apaches? Utes? Mexicans disguised as Indians? The captured women were never heard of again.

A troop of U.S. cavalrymen came to look into the raid. The soldiers and the women who showed up in their wake brought disease with them—measles, scarlet fever, smallpox. Many people died and many children lost their parents. In a roundabout way the soldiers brought hunger as well. They requisitioned corn, cabbages, onions, beans, and other foodstuffs that had been stored for winter use. They paid for the supplies, of course, but money didn't fill bellies for long, not at the price people had to pay to buy processed foods shipped in from far away.

The captain who led the cavalry troop had a sister in Michigan, who was devout but barren. When the Lord in His wisdom failed to answer her prayers to make her fruitful, she asked her military brother to bring her an Awahi child to adopt. The captain spread word that a good Christian home in

Michigan awaited some lucky child. He got no takers until the day the troop left the pueblo, when an Awahi man who had served the company as a scout and been dismissed for drunkenness brought the captain a screaming half-naked boy of about five or six. The former scout said the child's parents had died of the scarface disease and had no one to care for him. None of that was true.

"When Awahi women marry," the trader explained, "they keep their name and stay with their own families. If the marriage don't work out, it's the man who leaves, and he don't have no claim on the children or any property except what he brung with him to his wife's house. Children take the mother's name, not the father's. My own kids is Litukas, not Taylors. My wife, too. Don't bother me a bit. Point is, there ain't such a thing as a Awahi orphan. Kid loses his parents, his mother's family takes over."

The captain didn't know any of that. He gave the former scout a worn-out army blanket and a bottle of whiskey and named the child Richard on the spot. The boy was on his way to Michigan with the captain before anyone at the village learned of the transaction. In Michigan, Richard's new parents fed him well, taught him manners, dressed him like Little Lord Fauntleroy, and saw to it that he went to school and church, said his prayers, and washed behind his ears.

But Richard missed his home, his family, his friends, all the things and customs that made the world he knew. Awahi children were loved, fondled, and indulged by everyone in the village. In his new world children were regarded with suspicion. To his adoptive parents he was not just a frightened little boy but a bundle of devilish impulses, every one of which had to be suppressed to rip him from Satan's grasp. Bright and adaptable, he swallowed his resentment and learned all that was taught him. Learned, in fact, the trader said, more than he was taught. His teachers demanded that he abandon all he had known as an Awahi and accept new ways and beliefs. But in their struggle to change the way he looked at the world, his teachers unwittingly taught him skepticism. If what he had been led at Awahi to accept as God-given truth was false, why should he accept as God-given truth what Michigan now told him?

"Richard was a smart-ass kid, you see—begging your pardon, ma'am," the trader said. "Must've been hell to live with, a kid like that." By the time he was in high school there was nothing Richard left unquestioned, even the Bible. If it was sinful to believe that the gods led the Awahi people through four underworlds before they emerged at the Middle Place, lost their tails, and became people, why was it blessed and necessary for salvation's sake to believe that God created the world in seven days and made Eve from Adam's rib? Why not Adam from Eve's penis, leaving her just a stub? ("Begging your pardon again, ma'am.") It was not enough for Richard to be told that one way of thinking was sinful and the other was not. He wanted proof and refused to believe in anything that he could not see, taste, feel, or otherwise find a rational basis for.

He graduated from high school with high grades and thoughts of college. But he had grown so rebellious, so arrogant, and so disrespectful in his adolescent skepticism that his Michigan parents shipped him back to Awahi, a convert to cleanliness and rationality if not to Christianity.

"Can't blame 'em, I reckon, for washing their hands of him," the trader said. "They was nice believing folks and wanted him to be the same."

After all those years in exile, Richard was delighted to go home. But he found himself in a world he no longer knew. He discovered that Awahi was a wonderland only for the very young or very old. Children might be pampered and the elderly deferred to, but he was neither and not prepared for life as a young Awahi adult. His boyhood friends—those who had survived typhoid, smallpox, tuberculosis, meningitis, and diphtheria—had grown up experiencing rites and initiations that gave each a place in Awahi society as a member of one of the six kivas on which their religious lives centered and which were so sacrosanct that only the initiated could enter. An offense against the kiva—even an unsuccessful attempt by a nonmember to enter one—could be punished by death. There was no place for someone like Richard, who was ignorant of the rites that ruled adult lives and had never endured a yucca-whip initiation. He was a bystander in village life—Awahi born, but not Awahi.

John Purvis hired him as clerk and bookkeeper and found him a useful employee, though the young know-it-all could not resist lecturing his customers on any number of topics. He urged them to quit worrying about witches and start thinking about germs and good nutrition. He criticized Awahi men for spitting wherever they happened to be, even in the streets where children played in the dust, while also lecturing them on the benefits of fertilizing their meager crops with the abundant manure in their corrals. He urged women to boil the water they carried in pots to their families and to wash their nipples with soap before nursing their children.

Richard's contentious behavior upset the easy flow of village life, just when a long drought shriveled corn and turned grass brown. The river ran almost dry, and even the springs they had always been able to count on diminished. There was barely enough water for drinking, let alone for irrigating waffle gardens. The people thought, wondered, debated, and remembered that a long string of troubles had ended when Richard was taken to Michigan as a child. And now with his return troubles were again besetting them. They decided Richard was a witch.

"They was believers, too, you see," the trader said.

By this point in his story cigarette butts littered the stone floor at his feet, smoldering into caterpillars of gray ash.

"And then the wind died," the trader said.

Young members of the Warrior Priesthood, many of them buddies of Richard's in early childhood, took advantage of the rare moment when sorcerers lost their power. They seized Richard and took him before the village elders, who demanded that he acknowledge being a witch and accept responsibility for having caused the village's woes all the way back to the broken pots, the missing women, and his own kidnapping. Richard could have cleansed himself of the charges at once merely by confessing to evil acts and pledging to practice witchcraft no more. After an elaborate ceremony to drive out the spirits that had seized him and caused him to wreak such havoc, he would have been welcomed back to his former place in pueblo life, such as it was. Most witches confessed with no further ado. Richard refused. He taunted his accusers as superstitious savages.

They stripped him to the waist and put a rope around his neck. He was dragged through the pueblo, whipped at every step with sharp-edged yucca fronds. Each blow drew blood. In a small interior plaza reached only from the roofs of surrounding houses, the young men who had once been his friends wrenched his arms behind his back. Tying his wrists together, they hung him by a rope from a protruding peeled-log *viga* and pulled him up until his toes dangled inches above the ground. He screamed in agony as his weight pulled his backward-stretched arms from their sockets. Still he refused to recant, though he was savagely beaten with the yucca whips. Eventually, just short of death, weakened by pain and loss of blood, Richard confessed. He was taken to his mother's house to be nursed back to health.

It was about then that John Purvis hired Sam Taylor to

replace Richard and learn the Indian trading business. In time Richard recovered enough to keep the books and do light chores around the trading post. He was left sadly crippled, however, in the condition Quill and Jane had seen him earlier—barely able to lift his arms above his waist, with his spine so twisted that he could walk only by throwing his weight from side to side. He could speak only with great difficulty and communicated mostly in nearly indecipherable grunts and growls. He slept in a storeroom behind the post. Often at night, Taylor said, he rode his one-lung motorbike to the river, where he wandered along the bank, howling.

Chapter 10

In his office, filling out reports, Quill heard a light rapping.

"Come in," he called.

No one entered. The rapping continued. He got up and opened the door.

A towheaded boy handed him a note. He looked to be about eight or nine years old.

"Papa wants an answer right away, sir," he said. He spoke so softly Quill could barely hear him.

"Who is Papa?"

The boy looked astonished, as though he couldn't believe that anyone did not know Papa. Thick lashes guarded blue green eyes so bright that Quill thought instantly of the missionary. He said nothing.

"Come on in, son, while I read this," Quill said.

The boy stayed on the step. "Papa said not to, sir."

"That wind'll freeze your ears off."

"Papa said not to."

Quill closed the door while he read the note. It was addressed to "Brother Thomas" and said, "At your convenience I shall be there at ten o'clock sharp." It was signed, "Yours In Faith, Rev. Dirk Housma."

He opened the door. The boy lifted his eyes again. He looked as though he expected Quill to slap him.

"Are you sure this note is for me?"

The boy nodded vigorously.

"What exactly did your father say?"

"Papa said, 'Take this to the new principal. Be quick about it,' sir."

"Tell him fine. I'll expect him at ten."

By Quill's Elgin it was past ten thirty when the Reverend Dirk Housma burst in without knocking. He took off a fur-collared black overcoat as he entered, dropped it over the railing that divided the office, and placed a black fur hat on top of the coat. He was tall and heavy, bull-necked, florid-faced, with bulbous blue eyes—slate blue, Quill noted. He was a youngish man, little older than Quill, but already bald except for a closely cropped fringe of red hair reaching from ear to ear across the back of his head. His scalp stretched over his skull's dome, shiny as his high-laced black shoes. He wore a well-pressed black suit and vest, a freshly starched white shirt, and a string tie that had also been recently pressed.

Quill had barely got to his feet before the man was past the railing and upon him.

"Brother Thomas! Welcome to our fellowship in the Lord's vineyard of Awahi! Let us pray!" He seized Quill's hands in his and fell to his knees, pulling Quill down with him. They were knee to knee, nose to nose.

Quill strained to free his hands. The reverend held on tightly and prayed loudly. His hands were soft and damp, but his grip was strong. His breath was sour. Quill struggled to his feet, pushing Reverend Housma back on his heels just as he was saying, "And bless this new member of our Community in Christ."

"Get up," Quill said. His kneecap felt like it was pumping water, but he felt no urge to search for common ground.

Still on his knees, Reverend Housma gaped at him.

"Will you not pray with me, Brother Thomas?"

"My name is not Thomas, and I am not your brother."

"But Mrs. Wallis said a Mr. Thomas was coming."

"Mrs. Wallis got it wrong."

"I've never known Mrs. Wallis to—"

"Believe me, Reverend Housma. My name is Thompson.

"That does not alter the fact, Mr. Thompson, that you are here at godforsaken Awahi and I am delighted to welcome you in the Lord's name."

"Reverend Housma, let me remind you that this is a working office—a government office. There is a time and place for prayer, but a government office during working hours is not the place or time. Get up and get out!"

Housma struggled to his feet, bending to brush off his knees. "But I have business to discuss, serious business, the Lord's business."

"Then I suggest you get on with it."

"I came today to speak to you about your wife."

"My wife?"

"I am concerned about her."

"Concerned about my wife? What are you talking about?"

They stood eye to eye. Housma kept trying to press forward, almost bending Quill backward over the rolltop desk. Quill put up a hand, open-palmed, to fend him off.

"I fear she will be a dangerous influence in our community unless you are firm with her," Housma said.

"Take care, Reverend."

"I understand her maiden name was McGehee—Irish and Catholic!"

He exhaled in Quill's face.

Quill shoved him away. "You'll be happy to know, Reverend Housma, that though my wife is a McGehee, she is of Scottish descent, not Irish, and was brought up a Cumberland Presbyterian. But if she were as Irish as Pat and Mike and Catholic as the pope it would still be none of your business. So get the hell out of my office and let me do my work."

"You would speak to a man of the cloth in that disrespectful manner?"

"When necessary."

Housma sighed and shook his head. "I had hoped we could work together as Joshua Wilman and I did, especially since you're still favoring the missionary with his weekly meetings."

Quill had no idea what he was talking about. "I have no intention of favoring Sandringham in any way, and certainly not with weekly meetings."

"I am glad to hear that, for he is a gambler and a fornicator, not to be trusted. But Brother Thompson, let us not quarrel. Let us join hands as brothers in Christ to draw a heathenish people from their false idols and Rome and bring them to salvation. You can be a great help in our holy crusade."

He reached out as though to put his arm around Quill's shoulders. Quill again shoved him away.

"Are you proposing another attempt at grand larceny?" Quill said. "If so, let me inform you that should I find you with so much as one can of government mutton in your possession I shall put you under arrest and ship you off in chains to a federal magistrate. Which is what Mr. Wilman should have done."

"Are you threatening me?"

"I want you out of my office."

Quill's kneecap had long since quit pumping. He seized Housma's arm, whirled him around, and marched him out. Housma grabbed his hat and coat from the railing as he passed.

* * *

Jane was just leaving her clinic as Quill went to tell her about Housma's visit.

"I was coming to get you," she said. "The missionary is ranting in the hall and the whole school's there. Mrs. Wallis introduced him. I heard her warning the children to stand still and listen for the good of their souls."

"So that's what the SOB meant when he said I'm favoring the missionary!"

Quill tore open the door to the gym-auditorium in the school hallway. Children in red sweaters and gray stood in separate groups facing a platform at the far end where the missionary was in full voice as he paced back and forth, flinging his great black cloak about him and doing magic tricks. One moment he was drawing eggs out of his mouth even as he talked, and the next it was colored balls out of his ears. Mrs. Wallis sat at one side of the stage.

"I say unto you REPENT! REPENT!" the missionary raged. "The day of judgment is upon you and though ye be but a child GOD SHALL STRIKE YE DOWN! DOWN, I say, DOWN into the PITS OF HELL where you—yes, YOU, every last one of YOU—shall burn! BURN! BURN! FOREVER!"

Quill strode to the stage. Each step resounded like a drumbeat on the old wooden floors.

Mrs. Wallis frowned at him and put a finger across her lips. Quill saw but could not hear, "Shh!"

He turned to face the children and said, "Teachers! Take your children to their lunch. Reverend Sandringham, that will be all. I want you off the school grounds at once. Mrs. Wallis, I want to see you in my office."

Mrs. Wallis stood up. "Mr. Thompson, you have no right—"

"We will discuss this in my office."

The three young teachers herded their pupils out, heading for the dining hall. They smiled and nodded as they passed Quill. Miss Brewster added a surreptitious wave with a gloved hand. The children left quietly, faces impassive, but Quill saw more than one little boy nudging his neighbor.

The missionary followed Mrs. Wallis to Quill's office.

"How dare you!" Mrs. Wallis said. "You owe Reverend Sandringham an apology. And me, too. You have no right to humiliate me in front of the children."

"And you, Mrs. Wallis, have no right to invite a speaker to this school without my permission."

"Why, Mr. Thompson," the missionary said, "surely you're aware that Mr. Wilman arranged for me to give spiritual guidance to the children each week. I supposed you would wish me to continue. Think of their SOULS, Mr. Thompson. THINK OF THEIR SOULS!"

"I warn you, Sandringham. From now on you are not to come on the school grounds when children are present. Get out of my sight, both of you."

"Humph," Mrs. Wallis said.

She followed the missionary out, leaving the door open. Wind scattered papers on the rolltop desk.

* * *

From the start Richard Lituka proved indispensable in getting Jane's clinic set up and operating. Despite his physical disabilities, Richard seemed able to do all the lifting, carpentry, cleaning, and disinfecting required. He did much more as well. A quick learner, he was soon able to prepare a tray of instruments, organize the small drug cabinet, dispense medications, and keep the daily log. As for his sister Lina, Jane soon came to think of her as a friend, though she knew that the older woman would find the notion surprising. Lina treated her kindly and respectfully, but with a dignified reserve that never let Jane forget that she was an outsider, an intruder in Lina's world.

Fortunately, Lina talked freely about the behavior of her friends, relatives, and neighbors—especially when they did something she did not approve of, which was often. There was nothing about the village and its inhabitants that Lina did not know. Her lack of reticence even on such matters as what man was going to go home one of these days to find his paltry belongings outside the door of his wife's house gave Jane and Quill a view into the private lives of Awahi that they could have gotten in no other way. She was a sure guide for Jane and through her for Quill as they felt their way toward an understanding of the intricacies of Awahi life and culture.

One day Jane and Lina visited a member of the missionary's church, a woman named Mona Masuna, who had painful sores on her legs, making it difficult for her to walk. Mona was related to the family of Lina's husband, Ninsulka, the Rain Priest. Guided by Lina, Jane went to a narrow alley near the central plaza and climbed a ladder to the flat roof of Mona's house. Crossing the roof, they went down another ladder into a small inner plaza to Mona's door. When they started to enter, Mona refused to let Lina in. Lina had to stand outside Mona's open door, poking her head in just far enough to hear what was being said and shouting her translation, while Jane cleaned the sores and covered them with a soothing salve.

As they walked back to the school, Lina explained that Mona's animosity arose from a quarrel that spanned generations. Many years earlier, Mona Masuna's grandmother had put her grandfather's belongings outside her door after a vicious quarrel, thus ending the marriage. She refused, however, to give him a blanket that he claimed was his, but which she said was needed for Mona's mother and her other children, of whom there were a half-dozen. Mona's grandfather later moved in with a new wife, by whom he had more children, including Ninsulka's mother.

Mona was still quarreling with the descendants of her grandfather's second marriage over that blanket, the scraps of which had long ago gone to make a scarecrow and had finally blown away in a furious spring windstorm. Despite Ninsulka's position as Rain Priest of the North, Mona and her siblings and offspring would turn their heads when he neared and refuse to let their eyes see him. Nor would they speak directly to Lina or allow her to enter their houses.

They walked on in silence. Jane was not sure if what Lina said of Mona reflected the whole truth or just the detritus of an ancient quarrel. She decided that in some respects Awahi was perhaps not so different from a small town in West Texas or the U.S. Indian Service.

Chapter 11

On the last day of Quill's first week as principal, a northeast wind darkened the sky with dust clouds and sent skeletons of long-dead tumbleweeds rolling across the playground. As Mrs. Wallis prepared to conduct her opening ceremony, the wind flung sand pellets like flights of needles at the children lining up before her. They half-turned from her to keep the sand out of their eyes.

Mrs. Wallis blew her whistle. "This way, children—face this way."

The Awahi handyman—whose name, Quill had learned, was Juan Tsotomi—mistook the signal and at the whistle emerged from the building with the flag. Mrs. Wallis waved him back inside and whistled him out again when she was ready for the flag raising. Just as she raised the whistle to her lips for the Pledge of Allegiance, a child shouted, "Airpane! Airpane!"

The other children spun around and spotted a dot on the western horizon, struggling through the dusty sky against a powerful head wind. It was a biplane, one of those trying out routes to establish airmail service between Los Angeles and Kansas City. The planes had passed over Awahi several times before. Each sighting was an awe-inspiring event, but never before had the children seen a plane so low.

Breaking ranks, girls and boys in red and gray sweaters stretched their arms and flew over the playground like tumbleweeds caught in a wind devil. They banked and dived, making motor sounds and shouting to one another in Awahi.

"English!" Mrs. Wallis cried. "Speak English!"

The wind caught the flag and sent it snapping. Mrs. Wallis whistled furiously. "The pledge, children! The pledge!"

Mrs. Wallis's helmet of blondish hair loosened. Strands blew across her face. She whistled and waved her arms.

"Help me, someone!" she screamed. "Get inside, children. School is taking up!"

The children swooped and dipped, wings extended. The airplane dropped lower and lower, coming closer.

"Children! Inside this instant! English!"

Quill ran up the steps. "Mrs. Wallis, it's all right. We'll let the children watch the plane."

"The rules! Have you no respect for the rules?"

"Enough, I think. Now stop this."

Children spilled toward the gate.

"Keep them off the road," Quill yelled. "He's trying to land." He and Jane, along with the younger teachers, rushed to head off the children.

Gesturing wildly, Mrs. Wallis blew her whistle again and again. "Children! Inside! This instant! Inside!"

The biplane, held back by the wind and half obscured by the blowing dust, flew lower and lower, barely scraping over the cottonwoods along the riverbank.

"I don't know," Mrs. Wallis said. "I just don't know." She went into the school. The wind slammed the door behind her.

The missionary came loping across the bridge. His great cape swirled around him. When he reached the road and raced toward the school, he ran with arms stretched out in front of him, clutching a Bible. He looked as though he were about to take a running dive from a high board into a pool of dust. The wind hurried him toward the oncoming plane.

"EVIL, oh, EVIL!"

"Get out of the road," Quill yelled.

The missionary kept running. His bowler flew off, but he paid no heed.

"SAVE US O LORD FROM THE DRAGON CAST UNTO EARTH!"

The plane's engine coughed, died, caught, sputtered, and died for good. The plane, wings wobbling, floated past the Franciscan mission, dropping toward the road. It seemed to ride a wave, with its nose up one second and down the next. Quill could see the pilot peering over the side of his cockpit, trying to line up with the road and judging when he would drop down onto the straightaway.

The plane hit on one wheel and bounced onto the other. First one wing tip and then the other almost touched the ground. The plane hopped down the road toward the missionary, its prop spinning in the wind.

The missionary threw himself flat on the ground, holding the Bible before him.

"STOP! In the NAME OF OUR LORD! STOP!"

The plane slowed. Its tail dropped. The rear skid scraped along the ground. The missionary sprawled in the road, spread-eagled, with his wind-driven cape flapping over his head and his Bible held before him like a shield.

The plane stopped fifteen feet from him, its prop still spinning.

The missionary leaped to his feet. "A MIRACLE!"

The pilot clambered out of the cockpit. He was a jockey-sized man with a boyish face.

Children poured out the gate into the road and massed around the plane. The missionary elbowed his way through them. The wind wrapped his hair around his flushed face and under his chin like a golden wimple.

The pilot pushed his goggles up and unsnapped the helmet strap under his chin. His eyes were like the missionary's, blue green, piercing.

"Jesus, that was close," the pilot said.

The missionary waved his Bible at the pilot. "TAKE NOT THE NAME OF THE LORD IN VAIN!"

The little aviator looked astonished. "I thought you was in jail."

"Why would you think that? I have long since paid my debt to society for a trifling error and have returned to LABOR FOR THE LORD in this heathenish place, SEEKING SOULS TO SAVE."

The pilot staggered back.

"For Christ's sake, Uncle Tom, you'll deafen me."

"ON YOUR KNEES, BLASPHEMER!" The missionary seized him by the shoulders and tried to force him down.

"Uncle Tom! Don't you know me?"

The missionary peered at him. "Know you? But who, pray, are you?"

He looked again, more closely still. "Little Achie? Is that you? Brother Amos's little boy? Achie?"

"The same, but growed up now, Uncle Tom, and goddamned glad of it." The pilot pulled off his helmet and tossed it in the cockpit.

"THOMAS ACHILLES SANDRINGHAM III! Oh, Achie! ACHIE! ON YOUR KNEES! ASK FORGIVENESS! Your poor mother—THINK what she would say if she heard you!"

Achie twisted out of the missionary's grip.

"Save it, Uncle Tom," he said. "I've got work to do."

"And so have I." The missionary was weeping. "THINK, Achie, THINK of your IMMORTAL SOUL."

"You think about it, Uncle Tom. I've got to get back in the air."

Quill stepped in front of the missionary.

"Go along now, Reverend," he said. "You're interfering with the United States mail."

Tears left muddy tracks on the missionary's dusty face. Jane took his arm and guided him out of the crush of children. The tears stopped. Several brightly colored balloons, fully inflated, floated from under his voluminous old magician's cloak. As the wind whipped the balloons overhead, he clung to their strings with one hand while waving his Bible with the other.

"REPENT!" he shouted. "Oh, ye SINNERS! REPENT!" His eyes blazed. Hair flew like a halo around his head.

"Dirt in the gas line from all the junk I been flying into, I reckon," the pilot said. "I could use a stepladder, if you've got one."

Quill sent two boys to the shop for a stepladder, a canvas tarp, and ropes to create a shelter over the engine, protecting it from the blowing sand. Mr. Stilton, the maintenance man, came back with the boys, carrying the ladder.

The pilot brought out his tool kit from a recess in the plane's side. Clambering up the ladder, he removed the cowling, lengths of copper tubing, a glass cylinder, and oddments of the engine. He handed the pieces down to Quill and the maintenance man, who wiped them, blew through them, and—so far as Jane could tell—did all the things they might have done had the engine been in a Model T instead of an airplane. Their comments sounded the same, too.

"Looks clear to me."

"This nozzle's mighty fine, but probably don't signify."

"Little kink in this line. I'll just straighten it."

Achie Sandringham reinstalled the various parts. He checked joints, taped a few, tightened connections, and finally clambered down the ladder. He showed Quill how to spin the propeller without losing an arm.

"Like cranking a T-Model," Quill said.

"Something like," the pilot said. "But soon as you make the spin, jump out of the way so the prop or wings don't get you when I start to roll."

He stationed Jane at one wingtip and Mr. Stilton at the other, with instructions to steady the plane the best they could to keep it on an even keel as the engine caught. Jane had the added task of relaying his signals to Quill.

"I'll stick my hand in the air with the thumb up when I'm all set," Achie said.

He put on his helmet and scarf and eased himself into the rear cockpit. Mail sacks occupied the front cockpit, where a passenger or machine gunner might ordinarily sit.

The propeller was positioned almost straight up and down. Quill took hold of it, ready to spin.

Thumb up.

Quill pulled the prop around, pushing with one hand, pulling with the other.

Nothing happened. The motor did not so much as cough.

They went through the cycle from thumb up to spin a dozen times.

"Still not getting gas," the little pilot said. "The line's stopped up, I reckon."

He pushed up his goggles and climbed out of the cockpit. With the wind and sand still battering, he and Quill again set up the protective tent and prepared to repeat the process of disassembling, cleaning, reassembling.

The missionary leaned under the tent. Balloons disappeared under his cloak and so did the Bible. "Nephew, are you sure you're not out of gas?"

"Of course, I'm sure."

"Maybe we should check?" Quill suggested.

The pilot produced a yardstick from his cockpit. He poked it into the gas tank. He pulled it out and examined the end.

"Anybody here got gas?" he asked.

"The Lord will provide, Achie. The Lord will provide," the missionary said. As he withdrew from the tent he raised an eyebrow and smiled at Jane. He winked, as though they were conspirators in a shared joke and reached out as though to touch her.

She moved away from him and stayed close to Quill as he arranged for those with a car to give what gasoline they could spare to the missionary's nephew, so that the U.S. mail could be on its way.

* * *

Soon after the aviator was back in the air and the children were settled in their classrooms, Jane came to Quill's office.

"You'd better get over there," she said. "Mrs. Wallis has called a meeting of teachers in her classroom as soon as the children go to lunch."

"I suppose she has a right to do that," Quill said.

"Not if she claims to be acting principal while you are here in your office."

She showed him a note:

> I am calling an urgent teachers' meeting in my classroom as soon as we have taken the children to the dining hall for

their noon meal. You are to be there, without fail.

Irene Wallis, M.A., Acting Principal,
Awahi Day School.

"How did you get this?" Quill asked.

"Miss Brewster slipped it to me."

"I'll come to the clinic and wait there until it's time to join the ladies."

"I'll have the Mercurochrome ready to treat the scratches on your face," Jane said. "I've noticed Mrs. Wallis files her fingernails to a point."

* * *

Mrs. Wallis pushed the door open and with her back to the room held it for the other teachers. "I have an important announcement to make, and there is no time to waste," she said.

Leaning against her desk in the front of the room, Quill nodded and smiled at the three young teachers as they entered. They looked startled but said nothing.

Mrs. Wallis closed and locked the door. Turning around, she saw Quill for the first time.

"Get out!" she said. "You were not invited."

"That's true. But as principal of this school—"

"I do not acknowledge that."

"I am curious as to how and when you became acting principal."

"On Mr. Wilman's departure I was ordered by Mr. Thornton to serve as acting principal until a new principal arrived and took up the duties."

"If memory serves, Mrs. Wallis, I arrived at Awahi a week ago today."

"Oh, you arrived, all right. But you have not taken up your duties as principal. There has been nothing but chaos since you got here—no discipline, total disregard for long-standing rules, and serious violations of basic Indian Service policies. Today was the last straw. To lose nearly a half-day of instruction because of an airplane—unforgivable! I am sending Mr. Thornton a list, Mr. Thompson, a long list of everything you have done and failed to do. Until I hear from Mr. Thornton, I shall continue to act as principal of this school."

"Mrs. Wallis, this is insubordination, pure and simple. I was sent here to straighten out a situation that had repercussions all the way to Washington."

She interrupted. "Do not threaten me, Mr. Thompson. I know all about your friends in high places. I am not afraid."

"Nor am I, Mrs. Wallis. You mistake patience for timidity. I wanted to get familiar with the operations here before making changes."

"You have already made changes, basic changes. You have interfered with my efforts to maintain discipline and to provide the children with Christian guidance."

Quill turned to the other teachers, who had moved away from Mrs. Wallis. "I know this is difficult for you," he said. "But I want you to understand that despite what Mrs. Wallis says, I am in charge. I would be glad to hear what you have to say, on this or any other subject."

The three young women looked at one another.

"I thought it was wonderful for the children to see an actual airplane up close," Miss Tuttle said, with a sideways glance at Mrs. Wallis. "It opened up a whole new world for them."

"I think things have been running very smoothly," Miss Brewster said. "I have no disciplinary problems."

"Nor I," said Miss Ambler. "The children seem much less fearful than they were before you came."

"Of course they're less fearful," Mrs. Wallis said. "They know they can do or say anything in any language and no one is going to give them what they deserve."

"And what is that?" Quill asked.

"A good whipping."

"I disagree, but I won't debate you here. You are free to complain to Mr. Thornton or anyone else. But until my orders are cancelled, I am the principal of this school. I expect all of you, including you, Mrs. Wallis, to accept that fact and act accordingly."

"Humph," Mrs. Wallis said.

Chapter 12

Crossing the bridge to mail his report to Mr. Thornton on the day's doings, Quill saw the roly-poly Franciscan friar ahead of him, perched on the back of a burro that appeared to be resisting forward motion. The priest looked, Quill thought, as though he might be on the way to Canterbury. His brown habit and cloak blew around him. His pancake hat's earflaps were pulled down and held in place by strings tied under the lowermost of his chins. Stirrups dangled so far below the burro's belly as to make it appear that the Franciscan, short as he was, could put his feet on the ground and walk off his mount, were he so minded.

At the moment, however, the feet that should have been in the stirrups were kicking the donkey in the flanks. At every third or fourth kick, the beast put its head down and bucked, sending both rear legs straight out behind. Each time its hooves returned to the bridge they landed several inches ahead of the spot they had left. The result was a sudden arch of the animal's back, which thrust the priest powerfully skyward. He kept himself from being catapulted out of the saddle only by holding on to the horn with both hands and clamping the donkey's sides with his knees.

Quill overtook the priest as he was saying, "Now, Jenny, it'll do you no good."

"Good morning, Father," Quill said. "Anything I can do to help?"

Still holding tight to his mount, the friar turned his head and nodded a greeting. His head was round as a pumpkin and made up of circular elements—large brown eyes magnified by round tortoiseshell glasses, rosy round cheeks, and a round dumpling of a chin.

"I'm glad to see you," he said. "You must be Mr. Thompson."

"I am, and you must be Father Aloyisus."

"Forgive me for not shaking hands. I find it best to keep a firm grip when Jenny is in one of her moods. She's a good creature, but she doesn't care for this bridge." He risked taking one hand off the horn and patted the little gray donkey's neck.

"I don't blame her," Quill said. "I don't care for it either."

"Nor I. But if you wouldn't mind walking in front of her, she'll follow you. I think some previous owner must have struck her on the nose when she stalled like this. When she can see someone within reach of her nose she'll move quite smartly to fend off a possible blow."

Quill got in front of the donkey and stared her in the eye before turning his back on her.

"You've had experience with jackasses, I see," Father Aloyisus said.

"Mostly the human variety," Quill said. "But I grew up following a mule through cotton fields in Texas. Pretty much the same."

Once off the bridge, Quill walked at Jenny's side. Father Aloyisus had his feet in the stirrups again and one hand free. They shook hands.

"That was an exciting visitor who dropped out of the sky today," the friar said.

"It was. Our children got a lot out of seeing it, and I'm sure yours did, too."

People they met on the road eyed Quill warily but spoke only to Father Aloyisus, most of them warmly and some at length. Quill could not understand a word of what was said. But from sly looks thrown his way, usually accompanied by laughter, he felt sure that he was a principal subject.

"You must know everyone."

"You may say that. I have been here some twenty years—almost long enough to become accustomed to the wind."

Quill asked how long it had taken to become so fluent in Awahi.

"I started learning the language the day I got here, and I'm still working on it. It's a complex language. I'm trying to compile a dictionary. If the good Lord lets me live and my father superior continues to approve my pastorate, I hope someday to provide the Awahi with a written language. The people here aren't sure what the gods will think of that, but they allow me to keep edging along by instructing me in their language's intricacies."

At the trading post Quill waited while Father Aloyisus tied Jenny's reins to the hitching rail. The trader's compound shielded them from the wind, and for the first time Quill became aware of a sickening emanation from the donkey. It spoke of sewerage and ancient cadaver, with a hint of skunk and hair dampened by the ejaculation of vile fluids during unspeakable carnal acts.

"I see by your expression that you've noted Jenny's unusual fragrance," the friar said. "Years ago I complained to the mule skinner who sold her to me, but he told me, 'Ain't nothing but jackass. You get used to it.' And he was right. I hardly notice it until I see someone like you turning green after catching a whiff of her for the first time. Just try to stay to windward."

In the post Father Aloyisus and Sam Taylor exchanged comments in a flow of Awahi, in which Quill detected a few English words—among them "Wallis," "Housma," "the missionary," and his own name.

"The padre and me, we was just discussing the goings-on at your school the last few days," Taylor said.

Father Aloyisus added, "We admire the way you stood up to Reverend Housma and Mrs. Wallis, one after the other, and the missionary, too."

"I didn't suppose anyone knew about all that."

"News is the one thing that travels fast at Awahi," Father Aloyisus said. "Very little happens that doesn't reach the other side of the village in an instant. I think gossip's carried on the wind."

"Most of the time," the trader said, "the gossip ain't very kindhearted, especially when it's about whites."

"It's true we are often the butt of jokes," Father Aloyisus said, bringing out a pipe from beneath his habit. Lighting it, he issued fragrant clouds of smoke between words. "But I am constantly amazed at the forbearance these people display toward those of us who intrude into their ordered lives."

"They can get their backs up," the trader said.

"Of course. But look at what they put up with—they are shouted at by most whites, treated with contempt, and actively abused, and yet they find the grace to shrug it off. I sometimes think they are genuine saints. I wouldn't want my father superior to hear me say this, but sometimes I wonder if we shouldn't be letting them try to change us, instead of the other way around."

* * *

Before he left the post Quill asked Sam Taylor how to get in touch with the pueblo governor. "It's time I called on him. I should have done it before this. I don't even know his name."

The trader and Father Aloyisus looked surprised.

"You're the first Indian agent I ever heard of wanting to go see the governor," Taylor said. "Usually folks like you just send for him."

"Any reason I shouldn't go to him instead?"

"Nope. But a good reason to do it—he'd like it."

"What's his name and where do I find him?"

Father Aloyisus said, "His name's Kenoti. Wilman used to call him Ken, which the governor didn't like."

"What you had ought to do," the trader said, "just to do it right, is get together with Rain Priest Ninsulka at the same time. Wouldn't you say so, Father?"

"Absolutely. Then you're covering both religious and secular governance. Both are important here."

"Okay if Lina comes with me to translate?"

The trader and priest held a meeting of eyes.

"Not a good idea," the trader said. "Lina wouldn't go with you if you asked, and if she did go Ninsulka and Kenoti would get their noses out of joint. The men don't like women cutting in on what power they got, at least not out in public."

"I'll need a translator. Lina's taught me to say hello and goodbye, but that's about it so far."

Father Aloyisus said, "I'd volunteer, but I don't think it would be helpful to you just now, in light of the church-state issue that tripped up Wilman. But the governor and Ninsulka would probably be glad to have Sam speak for them, if it would be acceptable to you."

"I'd have no problem with that, if Mr. Taylor doesn't mind and it's okay with Governor Kenoti and Rain Priest Ninsulka."

"I don't mind," the trader said. "Just don't say anything to me you don't want them to hear. Not much gets past Kenoti and Ninsulka. Even if they don't speak English all that good, they know a lot more than they'll let on. These are two real smart hombres. That was something Wilman never caught on to."

As for where to meet, the trader said that was more difficult. Past meetings with village officials had always been held in the principal's office, but that wouldn't do if Quill wanted to make it clear that he was coming to them. Though they were the most powerful figures at Awahi, neither Ninsulka nor Kenoti had a fixed place of business where they met outsiders.

The trader said, "I can tell them you've asked to see them and invite them here. My wife'll feed them first—we do that all the time anyway. They feel comfortable here."

"When can we do it?"

"Best let them choose the time. That'll let them know it really is up to them whether to meet with you. Take a while to arrange. It's something new and they'll have to think about it and consult a lot of folks. The governor and Rain Priest can't get too far out in front."

As Quill left, the trader said, "Your wife was here earlier visiting my wife. I hear they got along real well."

"I'm glad to hear it," Quill said.

* * *

Earlier that day Lina Lituka and Jane had treated a man who had stepped in a prairie-dog hole while carrying firewood in a sling on his back. He fell sideways, twisting both his ankle and his back. Several sharp sticks had splintered against his side, drawing blood. Unable to walk and covered with blood, he returned to the pueblo draped like a sack of beans over his uncle's burro. Jane gave him aspirin, bandaged the ankle, and pulled long splinters out of his side, pouring iodine on the wounds, a painful experience that the man endured stoically.

On the way home, Lina took Jane to the trading post to meet

Flora Lituka, her sister and Sam Taylor's wife. At the trader's house Jane found herself in a large room that, pueblo style, combined kitchen, dining room, living room, workroom, and playground. It was filled with the latest equipment—chromed kitchen range, porcelain-covered water tank, oak cupboards with brass fixtures, a double-sized oak icebox, and a new foot-powered Singer sewing machine—but also featured a domed adobe oven in one corner. On the floor near the oven was a deeply grooved flat stone, a metate, on which Flora Lituka, like generations of women before her, ground corn for her family using a granite rock, a mano, in the immemorial Awahi fashion, stone against stone. Furniture in the rest of the room was as up-to-date and overstuffed as any in the latest Sears Roebuck or Montgomery Ward catalog, from which they had come. Bedrooms opened off a long hallway. Three of Flora Lituka's friends were there with any of their children who weren't in school—"kids all over the place," Jane reported, including three of Flora's four.

"I like Flora," Jane told Quill. "All those kids underfoot and her pregnant, and she's perfectly serene. She was really gracious about my just dropping in, and her English is better than Sam's. He came in for a few minutes, and he's a different man at home—kids run to him, climb all over him, pull his nose and ears, and he just wallows in it."

She added: "It was a good visit. I got to talk to them about vaccinations. Flora's children have all been vaccinated—Sam sees to that—and Lina said she thought the other mothers were interested. Flora invited me to stop in whenever I'm at the post. Lina said she meant it."

Chapter 13

That weekend Quill and Jane went to Gallup. For the Indian Service employees at Awahi and other reservations in that part of New Mexico, Gallup was "town," as in, "I'm going to town," or, "Next time you're in town . . ." People with money in their pockets could spend it on Coal Avenue, one block from Railroad Avenue—or, as was said in Gallup, "one block from Hell." J. C. Penney's, Piggly Wiggly, and the Ford agency were all on Coal and so were places to get their hair cut, teeth fixed, and suits cleaned. They could see a movie at a fancy new theater called El Morro, eat a noontime dinner or evening supper of chicken-fried steak, green beans, and mashed potatoes with gravy for less than a dollar at the Manhattan Café, with coffee and a slice of apple pie thrown in. For a dollar they could stay overnight on Coal—though on the fringe of town—in one of the new frame cabins at Constant's U.S. Auto Court, where the mattresses were clean and guests supplied their own sheets and blankets.

The only respectable establishment on Railroad Avenue was Fred Harvey's El Navaho hotel—redundantly called in Gallup "*the* El Navaho." The spelling was thought to be eccentric, intended to stop Eastern visitors from sounding the "j" in "Navajo." It was located at the Santa Fe depot, and when a train stopped to take on coal and water, passengers rushed for the lunchroom, where Harvey Girls in starched black-and-white uniforms offered a choice of three entrées available for instant serving. An overnight visitor could enjoy a leisurely meal in the more formal dining room. Here the tables were covered with spotless linens, and the Harvey Girls took time to present extensive menus that included fresh seafood, even oysters, shipped in daily from "the Coast," meaning California, aboard the Santa Fe's fastest trains.

Except for the depot and El Navaho, the buildings on Railroad Avenue stood across the street from the tracks. They were mostly one-story brick or frame structures, topped by false fronts decorated with soot-grimed signs advertising the saloons and dance halls they had once been. Railroad Avenue's better days had ended when the Volstead Amendment prohibited the sale of liquor and forced the bars and bordellos out of business or into signless buildings whose windows were blacked out with tar paper. Across from El Navaho one store displayed a crude sign meant to attract train passengers during a refueling stop.

Honest John's Pawn & Curio Shop
GENWINE INJUN CURIOS
STRATE FROM THE RESERVASHUN
HANDMAID!

Despite Prohibition, drunks sprawled on Railroad Avenue sidewalks with backs resting against the buildings and legs stuck out before them, openly nursing Mason jars of rotgut. Some slept, their empties beside them. The miners' strike was still on, and the National Guardsmen in full combat gear who paced back and forth along the sidewalk, rifles at the ready, had to step over sleeping bodies, sometimes kicking an arm or leg out of the way. Many of the drunks were Indians, which shocked Jane when she saw Railroad Avenue on their first Saturday trip to town.

"I didn't think they were supposed to sell liquor to Indians," Jane said.

"They're not supposed to sell to anybody."

"And no one stops them?"

"Not on Railroad Avenue."

* * *

They returned to Awahi on Sunday morning after a comfortable stay at Constant's Auto Court. There had been rain overnight in the low mountains between Gallup and Awahi, and a fast-moving snowstorm followed the rain, though the sky at Gallup was clear by sunrise. Jane had hoped to go to church while they were in town, but Quill insisted on an early start. He wanted to get past the steepest hills before the sun took the frost out of the ground. The Model T was heavily loaded, not only with their purchases and a sack of mail, but also with supplies for the school kitchen that they had picked up from a government warehouse—sacks of flour, onions, and potatoes, as well as No. 10 cans of mutton, green beans, and peanut butter. The backseat was stacked so high the springs barely held the car's body off the tires.

The Model T strained to reach the top of one winding slope after another. Near the crest of each hill Quill and Jane leaned forward in their seats, as though they could somehow will the car onward and upward. When they came to what was known locally as Ten-Mile Hill, where the road climbed by tortuous switchbacks along the face of a cliff, Quill said, "Time for a little fresh air." He stopped and unsnapped the window curtains on both sides of the front seat so that he and Jane could get out fast should the car start to slip off the road and down the cliff.

On the last sharp hairpin curve the car stalled. Quill let it roll backward down the narrow road, one switchback after another, to the bottom of the hill. He tried not to look into the depths of the canyon beside him as he leaned out to see where they were going. Jane warned him when he was about to run into the rocks on her side. By the time they reached the bottom, the brake linings smoked.

Quill said, "We'll have to go up in reverse. She climbs better that way."

"Will we have to unload and carry stuff up?" Jane asked.

"Hope not. We'll see."

"Shall I get out?"

"Not yet. I think we can make it this time."

As he guided the car backward up the hill, he was on the inside, next to the cliff, and Jane was peering down into the canyon, now alerting him when he got too close to the edge. Between them they were able to keep on the road, and the Model T labored to the top. Ten-Mile Hill was not the last before they reached the summit, but it was the only one they had to go up in reverse.

On the Awahi side of the mountain they felt that they had entered a new season. There had been no snow or rain there overnight. The wind was strong, but the sun was warm and the road dry.

"I'm hungry," Quill said.

He stopped in the middle of the road. Carrying a couple of blankets and their lunch—a thick round of gauze-wrapped longhorn cheese, with bread, apples, and two bottles of Coca-Cola—they climbed to a cavelike depression in the face of a cliff. It was sun-filled, sheltered from the wind, and overlooked a valley dotted with lava spires and walls left over from a volcanic past. The scene suggested the ruins of an ancient civilization.

"Our own little Eden," Quill said, as he checked for snakes. Finding none, he spread the blankets. They settled down to sip Coke and munch on cheese and bread.

Quill saluted Jane with his Coke bottle. "To surviving our first week."

They clinked bottles.

Jane said, "Has it really been just a week?"

"It's tougher than I thought it would be," Quill said. "I feel like we and the Awahis are on different planets. We live in our world, and they live in theirs. We want to make them like us, and they just want us to go away and quit bothering them. They have so little and need so much, and I have no idea what they need most. I asked Lina the other day what that would be. 'Rain,' she said. And without thinking I made what I thought was a little joke. 'The Rain Priest of the North will have to work harder,' I said. She shot me a look that said as clear as anything, 'You stupid man.' And she was right. I was stupid. I apologized. She just shrugged, as though stupidity was all that could be expected from a white man.

"And the children. I watch them come to school. They're lively and laughing coming across the bridge. As soon as they see me they look like convicts who've just seen the warden. I don't know what to do about it—and if I did know, I'm not sure I'm up to doing it. It's been a hell of a week."

"I think you've done pretty well, especially with Mrs. Wallis. She's what's wrong with the children."

"But a funny thing. You know how my left knee jumps and goes weak every time I think I'm going to have to argue with somebody? Well, that's how it was at the beginning of this week with Mrs. Wallis—Sandringham, too, and that other missionary. Housma, his name is. But I've accepted the fact that they can't be reasoned with—not any of them. They talk but they don't listen. There's no dealing with them. Confrontation is all they know. And my knee doesn't jump anymore. They're going to stab me in the back any chance they get, especially Mrs. Wallis. But I'm going to run that school the way I think it should be run, and the hell with them."

"Good for you!" she said.

He rolled over and kissed her. "How about an apple?"

She reached into the lunch sack.

"That's not what I meant."

"I know. But this rock is hard as a you-know-what, and it's covered with pebbles besides. I've got a sharp one sticking me in the spine right now."

"I could make a pad out of these blankets."

"Do you have a sheath with you?"

"In the car."

"By the time you climbed down there and back up again we'd both be out of the mood."

"We could take a chance."

"I don't think either of us would be happy if I got pregnant. Not at Awahi."

He lay back.

"I'll take that apple now," he said.

* * *

It was Monday morning, the beginning of Quill's second week as principal. The flag snapped in the wind. Rows of children, each row lined up behind a teacher, waited to march into the building.

"Lai-e-lai-tah," Quill shouted, standing at the top of the schoolhouse steps. He was speaking to the assembled pupils for the first time.

"Lai-e-lai-tah," he shouted again.

The children stood frozen. What would Mrs. Wallis do to the new principal for speaking Awahi?

On the steps below him Mrs. Wallis jerked her head each

time he said the word as though he had punched her in the ear. She said something that he did not quite catch. He felt sure it was not a pleasantry. As always, Miss Ambler, Miss Tuttle, and Miss Brewster seemed to act as one. They turned to look at one another over the heads of the children, smiled, and called, *"Lai-e-lai-tah!"*

He said it again, shouting it. *"Lai-e-lai-tah!"*

He beckoned at the children with his cupped hands, inviting them to respond.

It started with a couple of boys in Mrs. Wallis's sixth grade.

"Lai-e-lai-tah!"

Younger children picked it up.

"Lai-e-lai-tah! Lai-e-lai-tah!"

After a few moments of tumult, Quill motioned for silence. He continued in English. "I'm sorry I don't know more of your language, but I will try to learn, just as I expect you to learn English."

Lina Lituka stepped to his side and translated his words.

"I am happy to be at Awahi," he went on. "So is Mrs. Thompson, who has come to help you when you are sick." He pointed at Jane, who was standing in front of her clinic, her nurse's cap firmly pinned on her hair. The wind whipped her blue cape around her, providing glimpses of her crisply starched white uniform. She waved and smiled. *"Lai-e-lai-tah!"*

"I would like to say more in your language, but all I know is *Lai-e-lai-tah*. So I shall say it again." He paused and shouted, *"Lai-e-lai-tah!"*

The children shouted back. *"Lai-e-lai-tah! Lai-e-lai-tah!"*

* * *

He saw Mrs. Wallis coming across the playground to his office. She marched chin high and shoulders back like a commanding officer crossing a parade ground.

"Lai-e-lai-tah," he said, standing up at his desk as she threw open the door and stormed in, slamming the door behind her. He was glad to realize that his kneecap did not tremble.

"What do you think you're doing?" she demanded.

"Greeting you. *Lai-e-lai-tah* means good morning in Awahi—or good afternoon or just plain welcome, depending on the time and circumstances and the inflection you give it. It's an all-purpose greeting. I'm surprised you didn't know that."

"This is the last straw! Don't you know you are undermining everything we've worked for here?"

"No, Mrs. Wallis. I do not know that. And I believe this must be the straw after the last straw, which as I recall you said was the half-day lost to the airplane."

"Do you know what you've done?"

"Yes. I have taken charge of this school."

"Once again you have publicly humiliated me and utterly disregarded the rules and traditions of the U.S. Indian Service. I shall send another report to Mr. Thornton."

"I don't think anything you tell him about me will surprise Mr. Thornton or Mr. Lasher. Now please leave. I have reports to write."

"How can we enforce the rules and do our duty to God and our country with a man like you in charge?"

Quill said, "Mrs. Wallis, I suggest that you step very cautiously."

"Are you threatening me, Mr. Thompson?"

"I am warning you."

"Humph!"

She stormed out, leaving the door open.

* * *

A week later Quill had still heard nothing from Governor Kenoti and the Rain Priest of the North.

"Why won't they meet with me?" he asked Sam Taylor.

"That ain't it," the trader said. "If you ordered the governor to come see you, he'd be in your office right when you said. This is different. You asked to see them. They got to figure out what you might be up to."

Quill also hadn't heard from Mr. Lasher about Mrs. Wallis's complaints to Mr. Thornton, though mail had gone back and forth to Gallup almost daily during a week of relatively good weather.

"They're letting me twist in the wind," he told Jane.

"If that's so," she said, "Mrs. Wallis is twisting with you. Those two fuddy-duddies at Fort Frazier are scared to death of anything that might call Washington's attention to Awahi. They're just hoping that if they wait long enough we'll go away and they won't have to make a decision one way or the other. If they were going to back that witch you would have heard by now and we'd be gone from Awahi."

"Would you like that?"

"I want you to win, even if it means being stuck here. Not just because you're right, but because Awahi needs us."

Chapter 14

Winter ended with almost no snowpack on the Awahi side of the mountains, and the usual spring flood did not arrive that year. What should have been a raging torrent in the Awahi River as spring approached was nothing more than a series of puny rivulets idling between sandbars. The gales sweeping down the canyons to Awahi sucked the last traces of moisture from the ground and were stronger and steadier than Quill and Jane had known even in drought years at home in West Texas. No one could remember a drier, dustier time. Whenever Quill and Jane stepped outside into the sand-laden wind, they wore aviator goggles and covered their noses, ears, and mouths with scarves. When they got inside again, sand rimmed their eyes where the goggles had been. And even inside they could not entirely escape the wind. Fine sand filtered around windows and doors, formed mounds on the sills, and became an ingredient of every dish they ate. They could hear the gritty crunching as they chewed.

The freshwater springs on which Awahi had always depended for household use were reduced to trickles. In better times the women had used river water only to irrigate their waffle gardens. Now on many days women going to the spring-fed pools at the river's edge found nothing but wet mud. They were forced to shove sheep and burros aside to get river water that was thick with mud and filth. They let the muck settle before they offered the water to their families but resisted boiling it, as Jane tried to get them to do. They had never heard of germs. Jane reported that cases of diarrhea and even dysentery were showing up among infants and old people in the village.

"We've got to do something and do it now," Jane said. "I know regulations say we can't let the people use government water, but couldn't we at least supply enough for drinking?"

"Tell me it's a public health problem," Quill said.

"It's a public health emergency."

"We'll supply drinking water."

The school's water came from a vast aquifer that underlay the entire region. A small gasoline engine pumped water from a deep well to a steel tank that loomed over the school on thirty-foot metal legs. Water then flowed by gravity from the tank to every part of the school property. Mr. Stilton, the maintenance man, told Quill that it was a good system, but with limited capacity.

"We don't have no margin between what we pump and what we use," Stilton said, turning his head aside to squirt tobacco from a wad lodged in his cheek. He was a tubercular-looking man, so thin that seen from the side he seemed to have little or nothing between the front and back of his belt. "That's why Mr. Wilman, he had me shut off all the outside taps a long time ago. The damn Indians was sneaking in here at night stealing water. Wasn't no drought then—they was just too lazy to go to the river."

"Open the taps," Quill said.

"That little old pump ain't going to handle it. It'll burn out."

"Open the taps. I'll rely on you to keep the pump going. Give it a rest when you have to."

He took care to put a full account of his action and his reasons for it in his weekly report to Mr. Thornton.

* * *

One morning Sam Taylor told Quill that the Rain Priest and the governor had agreed to meet him at the trading post after Sam closed up for the day.

"Come by about six," he said. "The wife'll feed me and them and then we'll all talk. Won't take long. These folks like to go to bed with the chickens and get up with the roosters."

Quill planned to wear the workaday suit he had on to the meeting. Jane objected. The suit was an old pepper-and-salt of a greenish cast and did not fit. It bagged at the knees and elbows as well as, most notably, in the seat. Neither the sleeves of the coat nor the legs of the trousers were as long as they needed to be, while the waist was too big. The suit looked as if it had once belonged to a shorter, heavier man than he, though he had ordered it new from the Monkey Ward catalog, guessing at sizes, while he was still in school and just as thin and almost as tall as he was now. His shirt of brown and blue stripes fit no better. He wore it with the collar buttoned, without a tie, and his long neck rose out of it with room to spare all around. The frayed points of the collar curled upward like ski tips toward his chin. At one time, when they first met, Jane had tried to spruce him up, but dropped the effort. He had no interest in style and clung to the farm-bred belief that if he owned something it should be worn to the last thread, regardless of fit or condition.

But this time she said, "You can't wear that."

"Why not?"

"Because to them you represent the power and authority of the U.S. government. If you don't dress up for them they'll think you're telling them they don't amount to much. After this first meeting it won't matter what you wear. But this time it does."

Quill put on his good blue suit, along with a starched white shirt, a celluloid collar, his striped tie, and his kangaroo shoes, which he rubbed to a high gloss.

"You'll do," she said.

"I couldn't do more for the commissioner of Indian affairs," he said.

* * *

Two donkeys drooped at the trading post's hitching rail. Quill parked the old Model T well away from the burros and their battering heels. The blue white light of a gasoline lantern shone through the windows on either side of the post's triple-layered door. As he touched the latch a gust of wind pushed the door open and sent him flying down the steps into the bullpen. The lantern hanging overhead swung in the wind, sending grotesque shadows of saddles and washtubs flickering over the floor and walls.

Sam Taylor leaned against the front of the counter, rolling a cigarette. A bag of Bull Durham dangled by its string from his lips.

Quill tossed his coat on a bench and warmed his hands at the flat-topped stove in the middle of the bullpen. He pulled out his Elgin and checked the time.

"Sorry I'm late. The Ford didn't want to leave the stable. I about cranked my arm off."

"We been letting supper settle," the trader said. "This here's Ninsulka, Rain Priest of the North, and Governor Kenoti."

The two Awahi leaders sat on the benchlike ledge along one wall. Quill put out his hand.

"Lai-e-lai-tah," Quill said. "I'm glad to meet you, Mr. Rain Priest Ninsulka, Governor Kenoti."

They nodded but ignored his hand. Neither spoke. Both were short and stocky. Though they were about the same age, the Rain Priest's deeply lined face made him look much older than the governor, whose cheeks were plump and smooth. They both had black hair heavily streaked with gray, bobbed at ear level and held neatly in place by rolled bandannas. They were dressed as for an occasion in the spotless white pajamalike trousers that Awahis seemed to favor for dress-up, along with velveteen tunics. The Rain Priest's tunic was maroon, the governor's royal blue. Both were girded at the waist by concha belts. Their moccasins were deerskin, closed with silver buttons. Each man had a brightly patterned Pendleton blanket folded on the bench beside him.

The governor's trappings proclaimed importance. In his left hand he held a long wooden cane with a curved handle, more like a shepherd's staff than a walking stick. The wood was dark with age and had the look of burnished gunmetal. The cane was a mark of office, first bestowed on a native governor by the Spanish in the sixteenth century; it had been handed down ever since from one holder of the office to the next. Around Kenoti's neck a massive double-barred cross of hammered silver, also Spanish, hung from a braided leather thong. The governor kept what looked like a tight-lipped smile on his face, but his eyes remained alert and wary. Quill concluded that the smile was more a mask than an expression.

The Rain Priest displayed no special insignia. His massive squash-blossom necklace might have been seen on any Awahi man of substance. The same was true of his several strings of coral, bone, and turquoise nuggets. His eyes drooped like those of a man fighting sleep, giving him a careworn and weary look, as though he might drop off, unsmiling, at any moment.

The two Awahi men each opened a fresh pack of Camel cigarettes—given them by the trader, Quill felt sure. Striking matches on the stone floor, they lit up and smoked in silence. Finishing their first cigarettes, they each lit another from the butt of the first. They stripped unburned tobacco from the smoked-down butts and saved it in Bull Durham sacks that they produced from under their tunics. Quill lit up, too, and eyed the smoky patterns swirling in the harsh light of the Coleman lamp. Richard Lituka swept aside the curtain hanging in the doorway leading to the trader's stockroom. Hunch-shouldered and bent, he moved like an automaton on stiff legs and carried an oversized blue enameled coffeepot. It was steaming, and Richard wore leather gloves to keep from burning his hands on the wire handle. To Quill it seemed miraculous that Richard could carry the coffeepot without spilling, but he managed to lift it safely onto the stove.

"Thank you, Richard," Sam Taylor said. "You can go to bed now, if you want."

Leaving the gloves at the base of the stove, Richard lurched back through the curtain without looking at or speaking to anyone. He stopped just beyond the curtain. Under it Quill could see the worn toes and loose soles of his boots.

Sam Taylor took enameled blue mugs from a stack on a nail keg beside the stove. Putting on the gloves Richard had left, he poured four cups of coffee. For himself and the two Awahi men he added condensed milk from a Carnation can that for easy pouring had been pierced on the top in two places with an ice pick. He handed the can to Quill.

"You use this stuff?" he asked. "It's good for cooling it down."

"I'll skip it," Quill said. He leaned against the counter and sipped cautiously to avoid blistering his lip on the cup's hot rim.

"Let's get started," Taylor said, repeating it in Awahi, more out of courtesy than necessity. He hoisted himself up to sit on the edge of the counter, feet dangling. "Governor Kenoti, Rain Priest Ninsulka, you got anything you want to say?"

The two men appeared to ponder the question. After a long

pause first the Rain Priest and then the governor shook his head.

"Reckon it's your turn," the trader said, nodding at Quill.

Quill took his time. "Well," he said at last. "I am glad to meet you gentlemen." He spoke slowly and distinctly, knowing that both Ninsulka and Kenoti understood more English than they admitted. "I wanted to tell you that I don't know much about Awahi yet, but I want to learn."

Sam Taylor interpreted, and Quill continued. "I hope you will help teach me what I need to know."

He paused. The governor seemed to smile and the Rain Priest looked weary. They said nothing.

"One thing I would like to know is what you would like the government to do for the people of Awahi."

Pause. Silence.

"One thing I think the government might be able to do if you wish is develop a new source of water for you. The rains and snow of winter have not brought the water you need during this long drought. Your springs run dry on many days and the river is so low the water is like mud. Many people are sick from drinking bad water."

Pause. Silence. Ninsulka looked as though he might drop off to sleep at any moment.

"We at the school have a well that goes deep into the earth. We are sharing our water with you, but we cannot pump enough to give your people all the water they need. There is more water within the earth that we could reach by digging wells in the pueblo. Your women could fill their pots with sweet water whenever they need it."

Pause. Silence.

"I cannot promise that I can get the government to dig those wells for you. But I would like to know if you want me to try."

Governor Kenoti and Rain Priest Ninsulka sat smoking. They stared straight at Quill. He could not read the frozen smile on Kenoti's face or the weariness on Ninsulka's.

They stood up and clutched their Pendletons to them.

"Good-bye," Kenoti said, in English. The governor said nothing. He was no longer smiling.

They left, letting in a blast of frigid air.

"What'd I do wrong?" Quill asked. "Why did the governor quit smiling?"

"You didn't do nothing wrong," the trader said, "and that smile of Kenoti's—it ain't a real smile. I think it's a tic, or maybe somebody told him once that white folks like to be smiled at, so he smiles no matter what. It's like the Rain Priest looking sleepy. Far from the truth."

"Well, I'd have to say neither of them looked happy."

"You done fine. You made them an offer they're bound to like. But they're cautious—have to be, being who they are. They ain't going to make a move without they look it over like it's got fleas. If they wasn't interested they'd be telling you what a great man you are and how good your ideas is, but how—well, how maybe this ain't the right time of year to be talking about it. As it is, they've gone off to look at it in more ways than you and me can even have an idea of. They got to figure out what the gods think. Punch holes in the earth to get water the gods ain't already delivered? That's serious business. Not to mention that people here don't like change. It'll take time for Ninsulka and the governor to get their ducks in a row, but they'll be back. You can count on it. They need them wells and they know it."

"I hope I can deliver."

"I hope so, too. It'd maybe calm things down. I been hearing a lot about white witches lately. There's talk among some of the young bucks that it's us who's bringing all this bad luck—the missionary mainly, of course, but all of us. There's talk about driving white ranchers off Awahi land. Kenoti and Ninsulka is worried about keeping the lid on. The wells'd help."

"What happens if I can't deliver?"

"You'll be just one more government man who makes big promises and don't keep 'em."

"And if I can bring it off?"

"You'll own the place."

• • •

That night Quill stayed up late, writing a letter addressed to Thornton but knowing that nothing got to the superintendent except through Lasher. Mentioning the Indian commissioner's desire to hear no more of Awahi, he warned that the water shortage was inducing much discontent and foolish talk in the village. Tribal leaders were doing their best to calm things down, he said, but he would not be surprised if young members of the Warrior Priesthood tried to take matters into their own hands—which, he pointed out, would be bound to draw the attention of the commissioner, John Collier, the press, and Congress. Digging a few wells to provide an ample supply of potable water would be a relatively quick and inexpensive way to ease the rising tension. Finally he quoted a recent item in the Albuquerque Journal, reporting that Congress had appropriated emergency funds for digging wells and installing windmills on drought-stricken Indian reservations to provide water for livestock.

"The situation at Awahi is serious for both livestock and people," he wrote. "I request immediate authorization to proceed on the wells before we have an uprising on our hands."

Jane read the letter. "Devious," she said. "You make it sound as though we might be scalped any minute."

"I want to get Mr. Thornton's attention."

"You will."

• • •

Ninsulka and Kenoti finally sent word through Sam Taylor that there were doubters among their constituents who needed to be persuaded that it was a good idea to punch holes in the earth for water.

"I wish they'd hurry up and decide," Quill said.

"Ninsulka and Kenoti have to bring everybody else along. It's like a county commissioner getting a new road in his district. It's politics and pork barrel, like it or not."

At the trader's suggestion Quill invited the governor and Rain Priest to bring their doubting friends to the dining hall in early afternoon for, as he put it, "a bite to eat." On the designated day, twenty or so Awahi men crowded into the dining hall after the children had filed out. They took places on the benches, leaned their elbows on the table, and tucked into leftovers from the lunch Mrs. Stilton had prepared for the children that day. While his guests ate their canned mutton, stewed tomatoes, and hard tack, Quill gave a spiel, translated by Lina Lituka, about the convenience and value of pure water, emphasizing that care would be taken not to disturb the earth more than necessary. He used pictures and pantomime to show how the wells would be dug and how they delivered water.

As he finished he asked for questions. Sopping up the last traces of stew with hunks of bread, his guests looked at one another, rose, and departed. None asked a question—a sign, Sam Taylor said, that Quill was covering the issue just right and the pro-well faction was growing. The trader seemed sure of it, but Quill was not.

Ninsulka and Kenoti soon reported that they had encountered still more doubters. For a while Quill entertained several days a week, feeding as many as thirty or forty Awahi men at a time.

"It's a racket," he complained.

"Yep," the trader said.

No one attending the meetings protested Lina Lituka's presence, which was accepted as the price of an otherwise free meal. Sam Taylor said it was too bad no other women were present, because it was the pueblo matriarchs who most feared the changes that the wells would impose on the daily life of the pueblo. Getting the household water had been a woman's first task of the day, Sam said, ever since the Rain Priest of the North, having led his weary people up from the underworlds through which they had traveled for generations, spread his legs to pass his water, and announced, "This is the place." Going to a well and not the river or the springs would change the whole texture of life for the women, and they feared the consequences of seizing water where the gods had not offered it. What would the gods think? Water from the springs and the river was offered freely, like a mother nursing her child. Lifting buckets of water from a well would be like stealing it from the earth's unwilling bosom.

"The women," the trader said, "they're who you got to work on."

Quill pointed out that women were coming in droves to the school faucet. "Why's that water different from getting it out of a well in the village?" he asked.

"Because no Awahi was involved in that—that's a drilled well, and the drillers was white men from Gallup," Taylor explained. "If the gods was sore about your well, it's the government they'd go after."

Jane consulted Lina Lituka and her sister Flora and learned that it was they who had planted the idea of a meeting for women in the trader's head. Lina predicted a large crowd for such an occasion and suggested that the cooks prepare extra amounts of mutton stew and pinto beans that day. She also recommended that Quill stay away and leave it entirely to Jane.

"People like her," Lina said, making Quill ponder his standing in the pueblo.

* * *

Starting before noon on the appointed day, Quill watched from the windows of his office as women crossed the bridge in their best and brightest shawls, their legs wrapped in newly laundered leggings. The bulky layers of cloth made the women seem to be walking on fat stumps. Long before mealtime the playground was covered with groups of women sitting on the ground, shawls drawn over their faces as protection from blowing dust. Children too young for school but too old to be held chased one another and wrestled in the dust. As the waiting crowd grew, kitchen workers hustled to the warehouse to get more No. 10 cans of stewed tomatoes and mutton.

When the red and gray lines of children came marching from their classrooms to the dining hall, led by Mrs. Wallis's fourth, fifth, and sixth graders, the waiting women called to their children, who responded in a cacophony of Awahi.

"English, children!" Mrs. Wallis cried. "Speak English!"

Jane was with Quill in his office when the schoolchildren came out and the mothers poured in with their babies and toddlers.

"Well, here goes," Jane said. "Wish me luck."

"You'll do fine," Quill said.

* * *

The meeting lasted two hours. Now and again groups of women came out and went to the washhouse to use the toilets. Quill walked past the windows of the dining hall a number of times, but could see little more than long rows of women sitting on benches at the tables. All traces of their meal had been cleared away. He could hear bursts of laughter and cries of "A-yah, A-yah," which he took to mean approval of whatever was going on.

When the playground filled with departing bright shawls and romping children, Jane came to Quill's office.

"How'd it go?"

"Lina says you'll get your wells."

He still hadn't heard from Fort Frazier.

Chapter 15

As he sat at his office desk composing a renewed plea to Mr. Thornton for money to spend on wells, Quill glanced out his office window and saw a dusty limousine parked in front of the bathhouse. It was, he thought, the handsomest car he had ever seen and instantly recognized it as a sleek new—perhaps custom-built—version of the square-fendered Locomobile that General Pershing had used as his command car in France during the war. This one was a millionaire's town car, with curving fenders, a hood almost as long as a Model T, and two windshields—a folding one in front of the canvas-roofed chauffeur's seat and a second with its own electric wipers for the passenger compartment, which looked as roomy as a Pullman bedroom. Even dust could not dim the glittering radiator and headlights or the chrome that graced the wheels and accented every line.

A Pueblo man in a chauffeur's uniform sprayed the car with water from a hose attached to the faucet village women used. A bulky white woman in high heels, a big hat with a flower on the brim, and an old-fashioned motoring coat had a gloved hand on the faucet handle. A large reticule dangled from her free hand.

Quill rushed out of his office.

"Turn off that water!"

The woman ignored him. The chauffeur, one finger over the hose end to form a spray, continued to wash dust off the car.

Quill tried to get his hand behind the woman to reach the faucet handle.

"What are you doing, young man? Take your hands off me." She had the powerful voice of Quill's drill sergeant. "Don't you dare turn that water off! We left Gallup at dawn this morning and have been pelted with sand every mile of the way. I am surprised there's any paint left."

"Ma'am, you have no business on the school grounds," Quill said.

"Young man, do you know who I am?"

"I don't care who you are. You are trespassing on government property."

"I am Esther Olds-Chavez, and I am here on official business."

"Official business?"

"Well, important business. I have come all the way from Santa Fe at the request of John Collier and the American Indian Defense Association to take testimony from James McQuillian Thompson."

"Mrs. Chavez—"

"Mrs. Olds-Chavez, if you please. And who are you?"

"I'm Quill Thompson. I am principal of this school. I am sorry to be rude, but water is scarce at the moment. The springs have gone dry and so has the river. We are trying to supply water for the entire pueblo from the school system. Your car will have to stay dusty or some Awahi people will go thirsty."

"Don't you have wells? I see a water tower."

"There is only the school well, which is in danger of running dry. I have asked for money to drill wells in the village, but have not yet received it."

She bent and turned off the faucet. "Let the car go, Alfred."

The chauffeur looked at the last trickle of water coming from the hose. He shrugged and said nothing. By now the entire car was wet and glistening, all dust washed away.

"Mr. Thompson, I apologize. I had no idea the situation was so serious. Mr. Collier will be quite appalled. *I* am quite appalled. Where can we talk?"

On the way to his office, Quill took her to the clinic to meet Jane.

"Come join us," Mrs. Olds-Chavez said, issuing an order rather than an invitation. "You are involved in what I am here to discuss."

Mrs. Olds-Chavez seated herself in Quill's desk chair and directed him and Jane to straight-backed visitor chairs. She was a well-corseted woman and sat stiffly upright. A double string of pearls drooped into her lap over an impressive bosom.

"Mr. Thompson," she said, and paused. "And Mrs. Thompson. Mr. Collier has received disturbing information from a source who in the past has proved reliable about conditions at Awahi."

"Reverend Sandringham?" Quill asked.

She raised a gloved hand, forbidding interruptions. "Mr. Collier asked me to look into serious allegations made by his correspondent. These allegations concern both of you and other individuals as well. Many of the charges it makes are serious and if true will require immediate action on Mr. Collier's part. My part, too, of course."

"Of course."

"Mr. Collier is especially disturbed because, as you surely know, he was instrumental in placing you here at Awahi. He felt assured by what he knew of you, Mr. Thompson, that you share the aspirations of the American Indian Defense Association. He expected great things of you. Because of the trust he previously placed in you, he asked me to interview you about these charges."

Quill stood up. "Madam, this is highly irregular. If formal charges have been placed against me or Jane, it is a matter for the U.S. Indian Service and the commissioner of Indian affairs."

"A fool."

"Be that as it may, he is the responsible official. You have no standing—"

"Mr. Thompson, have you any idea who I am?"

"I know only what you have told me."

"I am an author, Mr. Thompson—and I may say without false modesty, a quite famous author. I am surprised that you do not recognize my name, because I have written extensively about Indian policy and am a founding member of the American Indian Defense Association. In fact, it was I who years ago interested Mr. Collier in the cause of justice for a mistreated, misunderstood race—a noble race, the original Americans, whom we have deprived of their land without adequate compensation. All too often we have deprived them also of their culture, religion, and lives, with no compensation whatsoever. When I speak, my voice is heard in powerful places. It will behoove you, young man, not to challenge my right to speak to you."

"Go ahead," he said, sitting down.

Mrs. Olds-Chavez opened her reticule and drew out several sheets of paper, which she laid on Quill's desk.

Taking up the top sheet, she said, "This page concerns you directly. It is a copy, somewhat abbreviated, of charges made against you."

She handed the sheet to Quill. It was typewritten and headed at the top "Excerpts." It bore no name or other indication of its source, but many words and phrases were written in capitals.

"Ah, yes, the missionary," Quill said.

"The missionary?"

"Sandringham. He speaks and writes in capital letters. You can't mistake it, assuming that this is an exact copy."

"It is."

The excerpt read: "Sometime ago you sought to clear up a disturbing situashon at Awahi Indian School. It is TIME to ACT again. You will find on taking charge of the school the new principle Mr. James McQuillan Thomson has refused to follow RULES and REGULATIONS. He lets YOUNG HEATHENS speak UNCHRISTIAN TONGUES during SCHOOL HOURS and on SCHOOL GROUNDS and has STOPPED whipping pupils who vilate rules LEADING TO ANARKY. He REFUSES to let a PROTESTANT MINISTER preach the TRUE WORD OF GOD to children HUNGRING FOR SALVATION but entertains GODLESS SAVAGES with GOVERMENT FOOD to promote his own schemes. All this IS FULLY DOCMENTED."

"Mr. Thompson, is this true?"

"Well, I'm not sure about the 'anarky,' the hunger for salvation, and godless savages—the Awahis I know have more gods than you can shake a stick at. But essentially, yes. I plead guilty. Those are things I have done or refused to do. "

"Good," Mrs. Olds-Chavez said. "Mr. Collier will be relieved."

"But why would Sandringham send this to Mr. Collier and not, say, to Mr. Thornton at Fort Frazier or the commissioner?"

"These allegations were contained in a carbon copy of a letter addressed to Mr. Thornton. We believe it may have been sent to us by mistake. We are, of course, grateful for the error, if it was an error, since it suggests that you are attempting to run Awahi in a sensible manner."

She handed over three more pages. The first opened: "With the CURRENT PRINCIPLE came his wife Jane a nurse. She set up a clinic to meet the HEALTH NEEDS of the Awahi people and treats not just children who attend the government school but Pupils being fed the POISEN OF ROME at the Franciscan mission. THEY LIVE IN FILTH and are as IGORNANT of sanitation as they are of TRUE SALVATION."

After that relatively harmless introduction, the missionary accused Jane of being both a "PAPIST" and an "ABORSHUNIST," naming two women and giving dates. "BOTH THESE WOMEN is willing to tell THEIR STORIES and is determined to STOP THIS MURDERER from KILLING INNOSENT AWAHI UNBORN BABIES."

"He's just plain lying," Jane said. "Both women miscarried and had complications. I had nothing to do with inducing the miscarriages but treated the aftereffects." She also pointed out that abortion was not part of the Awahi culture, in which every child was welcomed, even those born deformed.

"Let's get Lina and go see the women," Jane said. "They won't lie."

"Of course," Mrs. Olds-Chavez said, "but first we should consider charges against Mr. Samuel Taylor, an Indian trader, and Father Aloyisus at the Catholic mission. I want to see them as well."

About the trader, the missionary wrote, "Samuel Taylor and his employ Richard Lituka has vilated the law by selling ALCOHOLIK BEVERAGES on his trading premises to members of the Awahi Indian tribe. Two LOYAL CHRISTIAN members of my mission church will SWEAR that Taylor TRIED TO SELL them liquor."

The missionary added that he stood ready to "TAKE OVER operation of the AWAHI TRADING POST if you will revoke

Sam Taylor's license and issue it to me and will operate it as a TRUE CHRISTIAN ENTERPRIZE."

"I can vouch for Sam," Quill said.

"We'll let him speak for himself," Mrs. Olds-Chavez said. She moved on to the case of Father Aloyisus:

"Altho I know you have no sympathy for ROME I believe you will be shocked to learn that Father Aloshus A FRANCISCAN PRIEST has vilated all terms of HUMAN DECENSY AND MORAL CONDUCT by consorting with and misbehaving with young boys and girls. Members of my congregation are prepared to SWEAR TO THESE MATTERS if you determine to look into them." The letter continued with allegations that Father Aloyisus had failed to carry out his priestly duties and had learned HEATHEN RITES in order to incorporate them into the Christian liturgy and "has been RELIABLEY reported to preach in the PAGAN tongue!"

"Now let us go see Mr. Taylor and Father Aloyisus," Mrs. Olds-Chavez said. "I do not think we need trouble the poor women about their miscarriages."

They drove in the Locomobile. Jane sat with Mrs. Olds-Chavez in the passenger compartment, where, she later reported, there were silk flowers in vases beside each door and a heater to warm one's feet. Quill, reveling in the roar of the vehicle's multi-horsepower engine, sat beside the chauffeur, who introduced himself as Alfred Chavez. He spoke excellent English and was full of details about horsepower, torques, and gears. He offered to let Quill drive.

"My wife won't mind," he said. "She likes to show it off. So do I."

"I wouldn't dare," Quill said. He wanted to ask how much the car cost, but didn't.

* * *

"The son of a bitch!" Taylor said, without apology. He added, "It ain't true, you know. I ain't never dealt in booze. Wouldn't stand for it. And even if I wanted to, my wife wouldn't let me. But what's true or not true don't matter. If he spreads this around there's bound to be an investigation and by the time it's over I'll be so smeared life won't be worth living. It'll be a miracle if I keep my trading license."

* * *

"That's a lie!" Father Aloyisus said. His face, always flushed, turned as red as if someone had just daubed his cheeks with rouge. "Corrupt my children? I've done no such thing! And I have had my order's permission and encouragement in my studies and use of Awahi culture and language. But true or not, if these charges were ever to become public I'd be shifted somewhere else." He added, "I'm useful here and comfortable besides."

* * *

Jane asked Mrs. Olds-Chavez and her husband to have lunch with them. Mrs. Olds-Chavez declined for both.

"We carry our own provisions," she said. She added, "We shall be at El Navaho in Gallup tonight. I shall stop at Fort Frazier to meet with Mr. Thornton early tomorrow on the way back to Santa Fe."

Quill and Jane stood waving as the Locomobile moved out of the school compound.

"What a car!" Quill said. "I bet it cost ten years' salary."

"What a woman!" Jane said. "I wouldn't want to meet her in a dark alley."

Chapter 16

Quill was at the trading post chatting with Sam Taylor when a coal-truck driver dropped off the mail. The usual delivery came in a limp gray sack that had so little in it—a handful of letters, a magazine or two, and a few days' issues of the *Albuquerque Journal*—that it slumped on the floor like trousers without legs in them. But this time the mail filled two sacks so stuffed and heavy that the driver had to bring them in from his truck one at a time, and when he put them down they stood upright on their own bottoms.

"What's all this?" Quill asked.

"The missionary," the trader said. "I reckon the probation he got put on when he left Leavenworth must be up and he's gone back to his old money-raising tricks. He sent out a big batch of begging letters a while back. These here sacks is filled with envelopes addressed to Sandringham. Lots of 'em'll have dollar bills or checks in them, and the rest will have coins rattling around."

"Doesn't he risk going to jail again?" Quill asked.

"It's legal enough, long as he don't pass himself off as somebody else, like he done before," the trader said. In the money-raising foray that brought his downfall, Taylor explained, the missionary was working as an assistant to the Reverend Andries Ryenger, the uncle of Reverend Housma and founder of the

Reformed Church of the New Beginning Mission at Awahi. Ryenger was impecunious and so was the Michigan sect that had sent him to minister to the heathen Awahi. It was up to him to support himself and his mission by using the U.S. mails to beg money from members of the Reformed Church of the New Beginning in America.

"Old Ryenger," Taylor said, "got so he could whistle a dime out of a starving man's pocket with the letters he wrote. He could make his little mission sound like the Alamo, surrounded by bloodthirsty heathens and only him holding them off with one hand while trying to save their souls with the other. How's he going to get all them misguided Injuns to Salvation and out from under Father Aloyisus's heel if folks don't pony up the wherewithal? Read one of them letters and you'd be emptying your purse and asking him was it enough to protect him from them howling savages that Rome—Father Aloyisus, he was talking about—was sending to attack his little mission. Every month or so he'd send off a batch of letters, and the envelopes stuffed with coins and bills would come pouring back."

After the missionary went to work for Ryenger he became almost a member of the family—"maybe more so than the Reverend knowed," Taylor said—and took over many of his mentor's chores. Mastering the art of the begging letter under Ryenger's tutelage, he soon proved even more adept than his tutor at describing hairbreadth escapes from howling savages, godless desperadoes, rapacious Roman Catholic priests, and miraculous conversions made possible by the God-fearing donors to Ryenger's mission.

The trader brought out two letters that the missionary had written on Ryenger's behalf. Taylor said he had found the letters, without envelopes, on the bullpen floor after a mailing. The first letter opened with a description of the Ryenger family's arrival at Gallup on the way to Awahi many years earlier. It was an event that Ryenger had frequently used in his begging, but one Sandringham embellished:

> "Now my Dear Bros. In Christ think of a black beard man dressed in lether named BAD BRAD JAMES and around him no one but THUGS. Think of six-guns big as shotguns and all pointed at your HEAD. Your dear WIFE AND BABES. Too. Think of a voice like gravel and a bottle of the DEVIL'S BREW in every hand. And the voice growls DANCE FOR YOUR LIFE Padre! And FIRES A GUN at your feet! Dust and gravel fly up in the face of your preshus wife and bairns.
>
> Oh, Dear Friend, WHAT ARE YOU TO DO? With death looking you in the face, what but PRAY? Dear Lord FORGIVE These Men, I cry, for they know not what they do! And I hold out the GOOD BOOK to Bad Brad James and the DESPERADOE FALLS ON HIS KNEES and with tears in his eyes ACEPTS CHRIST!!! A MIRACLE!!!
>
> Your PRAYERS and GIVING made it HAPPEN!!! Dear Bros. In Christ, there are MIRACLES YET TO COME at benighted Awahi and YOU CAN MAKE THEM HAPPEN TOO! Open your HEARTS and POCKETBOOKS again DEAR BROS. IN CHRIST and send your mite to our Holy Mission and MAKE A MIRACLE. YOU CAN SAVE THE SOUL OF YET ANOTHER HEATHEN!!!

The missionary's other letter to Ryenger's contributors told the dramatic story of Uncle Andries' reception as he and his family first reached Awahi.

On that Blessed Day when I first saw the anshunt village of Awahi my heart sunk LIKE LEAD IN MY BREAST. I saw filth in the streets and the children running NAKED not just boys but GIRLS not a stitch! SHAMELESS! We came in wagons drawn by mules. Came without guns though told of the dangers we faced armed only with THE GOOD BOOK and LOVE IN OUR HEARTS. Miles from the village runners dart over the land before us. Naked grown men NAKED racing barefoot over cactus. My sweet wife turns her pure head and MY SWEET BARNS too.

As we grow near the village we come to a GREAT DRY RIVER. On the far side a vast throng rushes out. To greet us we expect. BUT NO! Painted savages in hidous masks Carrying SPEARS! Bows! ARROWS! GUNS!! And behind them what do we see? ROME! We see ROME!! PRIESTS lurk behind them! Hoods to hide their faces! WE SEE THE HAND OF THE POPE!! His DRED FACE!!!

What to do? How to protect MY LITTLE FAMILY from a TERRBEL FATE at the cruel hands of ignorant HEATHENS abeted by ROME?

The DEVIL'S HORDES RACE across the dry sands of the river! I FALL TO MY KNEES! I hold UP my Bible To the Lord. SAVE US, O LORD! I cry. SAVE YOUR FAITHFUL SERVANT! And LO! A great roar like a thousand locomotives! A WALL OF WATER rushes down the river and DROWNS OUR ENEMIES! The people of the village RUSH TO GREET US. HELP US they cry. SAVE US FROM ROME AND THE DEVIL!!!

And THINK dear Bros. In Christ without your necessary gift this MIRACLE, for A MIRACLE is what it IS, could not happen. WE THANK THEE IN THE SAME BREATH

> AS GOD! And will you not LOOK INTO YOUR HEART and send another mite for this mighty task of bringing CHRIST to Awahi? YOU TOO CAN MAKE A MIRACLE!! Dig deep IN YOUR PURSE Dear Bros in Christ. MAIL IT TODAY for SWEET JESUS and your own PLACE IN HEAVEN!!!

"I think I could hang on to my dime," Quill said.

"Mebbe so, but a lotta folks didn't," Sam Taylor said. "I think it was all them capital letters done the trick. They was like passkeys to people's pockets."

He paused to roll a cigarette. "Anyway, the missionary keeps sending out letters, but all of a sudden nothing's coming back, not a dime—at least, not to Ryenger. The old boy comes in here all but bawling like a baby. He has a payroll to meet, a big family of children to feed. Has to put clothes on their backs, too. But that river of money he's been fishing in for years has dried up. The Lord has turned his back on him, and he don't know what to do.

"I can't help feeling sorry for him, and I tell him that the missionary has done gone into business for hisself. He's sending out the same begging letters Ryenger showed him how to write. But now the answers and the money is coming back to Sandringham at the Church of Jehovah's Sweet Light of Jesus Mission instead of to Ryenger at the Reformed Church of the New Beginning. Ryenger says, 'The Church of Jehovah's Sweet Light of Jesus Mission? What's that? I never heard of the Sweet Light of Jesus Mission.' I tell him it don't exist at the time except as a mailing address, but the missionary has got the old fella who was governor then to give him land to build on. 'Behind my back,' Ryenger says, 'behind my back!' And he goes outta here using words I didn't reckon a preacher would know."

What happened then, the trader said, became common knowledge and was relished by the gossip-loving villagers. Whatever else he was—unworldly, gullible, vain, bombastic, and incurably devious—Reverend Ryenger was a fighter. He rushed through the heat of August from the trading post straight to the governor, a predecessor of Kenoti. He found the old man at his usual post in the central plaza, sitting on the ground, leaning back against the wall of his daughter's house, his legs outstretched before him, dozing in the hot afternoon sun. The governor was in his early fifties, ancient by Awahi standards, and had long since mastered the necessary art of extracting what he could for the village treasury from Anglo intruders. He was deaf, half-blind from trachoma, and in the last stages of tuberculosis. Warm as it was, he had a green, black, and yellow-striped Hudson's Bay blanket, a bit ragged on one edge but still serviceable, draped around his shoulders.

Ryenger squatted. He was a big-stomached man and did not find it easy to get his haunches to his heels. "Governor," he shouted. "Let us pray."

The governor lifted one hand, consenting, but before Ryenger could get started the governor's daughter came to the open door of her house, wearing a green cotton housedress she had made on Singer sewing machines at the government school, using material and a pattern supplied by the nuns at the Franciscan mission. Not bothering to get her tongue around "Reverend Ryenger," she said, "Go on, Revenger, he awake."

"Our Father," Ryenger roared. With the daughter translating, he enumerated a long list of Heavenly favors bestowed on Awahi and the governor through his intervention. He singled out for special mention the governor's three-striped Hudson's Bay blanket, which had been donated by one of Ryenger's Michigan supporters.

After a couple of minutes, he got to the crux of the matter: "And finally, O Gracious Lord, help us to know our friends and protect us from those who speak with false tongues. In particular, Lord, nurture the efforts of your humble servant Reverend Ryenger to bring your Sacred Word to the poor savages at Awahi, who thirst for News of Salvation. Let thy Grace descend on the governor and his council as they consider the nefarious application to give up precious Awahi land to the false missionary Sandringham Jr. Guide them in their deliberations! Let them remember that Reverend Ryenger is the one who supplies the esteemed governor of Awahi with a dollar a month for his service to the Lord as chairman of the Board of Native Advisers to Reverend Ryenger. We pray, O Lord, that you make the governor understand that Reverend Ryenger will be unable to give him money every month if the governor gives land to the Reverend Sandringham Jr."

At this point, Ryenger ended with an abrupt and emphatic, "Amen!"

With scarcely a pause he thrust his face inches from the old man's nose, stared him in the eyes, and demanded, "All right, Governor, how much did he pay you?"

The governor lifted one hand and put up two fingers.

"Two dollars?"

The old man nodded.

Ryenger took five one-dollar bills out of his purse and smoothed them out. "I'll give you a five-dollar bonus for your past service as chairman of our Board of Native Advisers. Keep up the good work and I'll be by next week with your regular stipend. You want the dollar a month to continue, I'm sure."

The governor's daughter spoke for him. "Revenger, sir. My father, he like dollar ever month. Two dollar, my father, he like better."

Ryenger struggled to his feet. "Two dollars it is. Get that land back from the missionary. Bless you both," he said. He turned homeward with the air of a man who has done a good afternoon's work and is confident that the Lord will smile on a faithful servant who felt the need to refresh his corporal being with a nap.

When Reverend Ryenger, sleepy-eyed, entered his house after his negotiations with the governor, his ears were prepared only for blessed silence. His wife and daughters were over at the school, preparing for the imminent opening of classes for a new year, and he expected to be alone in the house except for the servants, who didn't count. Instead of silence, he was greeted by moans and gaspings of an unseemly sort, many uttered in masculine tones and emanating from his eldest daughter's room. He rushed down the hall and crashed through the door. Thrashing on the bed in a tangle of bare arms and legs were his daughter Aafka and the Reverend Sandringham Jr.

"Ah," Quill said, when the trader reached this point in his narrative. "The Housma boy with the missionary's eyes."

"You got it. Well, Ryenger hustles Aafka off to Michigan and marries her to Housma, his nephew, who's just out of the seminary. In return Housma gets him a pretty wife, a son in the oven, and a moneymaking mission all set up and running. And the missionary goes to Leavenworth for mail fraud."

"I've never seen Housma's wife," Quill said.

"You ain't likely to. Watches her like a hawk, Housma does. Folks who work for him say he sees the missionary behind every bush. He's got him a big wide belt hanging on the back of a door. Uses it on her regular. His kids, too, especially that boy with the missionary's eyes."

* * *

The truck driver who brought the two sacks of mail to the missionary also delivered a note from Mr. Lasher to Quill and a manila envelope stamped "Confidential." The note informed him that Mr. Thornton had approved his proposal for water wells and authorized him to spend up to five hundred dollars on four wells in the village using local labor.

The manila envelope contained letters Mrs. Wallis had sent to Mr. Thornton. With the letters was a second note to Quill on official stationery from Mr. Lasher. "Please advise Mrs. Wallis that Mr. Thornton acknowledges her reports about the state of affairs at Awahi. Her letters are enclosed for your files or for return to her, at your discretion. As for her request for transfer, please advise her that he would prefer that she resubmit it at an appropriate time."

Quill had not known that Mrs. Wallis had requested a transfer and couldn't help wishing that she had been granted it. But what did "an appropriate time" mean? He had no idea.

Quill took her letters and the note to Mrs. Wallis after school. She sat at her desk with an Oriental-patterned shawl over her shoulders. She had complained about drafts ever since Quill had instructed Mr. Stilton to pull the nails that had kept the windows closed.

"Mr. Lasher sent these for me to give to you," Quill said.

She seized the packet of letters, read the note, and thrust both the note and the packet in a desk drawer.

"You had no right to read these letters," she snapped.

"True, and I did not."

"I don't believe you."

"I can't help that."

He walked out before she could get out a "Humph."

Chapter 17

Ninsulka and Kenoti still had not approved the water wells. Sam Taylor advised Quill not to tell them that he had received authority to start digging.

"Save that until after the governor and Rain Priest say they want the wells," the trader said. "That way they can claim credit for them."

A few days later the governor and the Rain Priest came without notice to Quill's office. They smoked a half-dozen of his cigarettes and informed him through Lina that they would welcome the wells, provided that the proper ceremonies to square things with the gods were held before work began and again before the first water was lifted from the earth.

Quill declared a school holiday for the day that work on the first well was to start. A crowd gathered early. Men stood against the walls of the small plaza that had been picked as the site. Some dangled their legs over the edge of second-floor terraces. Women sat in doorways, on the edge of communal domed ovens, and on the ground with shawls spread around them. Babies slept or nursed in their mothers' arms and toddlers gamboled underfoot. Older children in red and gray school sweaters were everywhere. The sky was browned by windblown dust, but the square, located deep within the pueblo, was protected from the wind by the stacked houses surrounding it.

"'Ello, 'ello," children called as Quill and Jane found places at one side of a doorway. Miss Ambler, Miss Tuttle, and Miss Brewster, but not Mrs. Wallis, entered the square a few minutes later, also to a chorus of 'ellos. Quill saw Sam Taylor and Father Aloysius standing together across the way. There was no sign of the missionary or Reverend Housma. A faint drumming sounded in the distance. As it grew closer, tinkling bells and the sound of flutes joined the drums. From a rooftop overhead came the cry, "REPENT, ye SINNERS! REPENT!"

Three mud-smeared clowns, naked except for loincloths and their baked-clay masks, struggled with the missionary as he started down a ladder.

"THE LORD COMETH!"

The mudheads hauled him off the ladder into the square. He towered over them, but in the tussle one clown managed to knock off his bowler. A gust of wind seized it and sent it flying into the sky.

"FORGIVE THEM, LORD. They are but SAVAGES AND KNOW NOT WHAT THEY DO!"

A mudhead got on his hands and knees behind the missionary. The other two pushed from the front, and he fell backward. Onlookers laughed and cheered. The mudheads held him down, muffling his cries.

"SAVAGES! HEATHENS! INFIDELS!"

More mudheads poured into the square, prancing and cavorting through the crowd. They grabbed men and women indiscriminately and, to cheers and laughter, pretended to have brief sexual encounters. One came up to Jane, put a hand on her shoulder, and then backed away, shaking his head and smacking the hand away from her shoulder with his other hand. The crowd howled with laughter. As the clown passed on, Jane curtsied. The crowd cheered.

After the mudheads a line of dancers wearing only grotesque masks and kilts entered the square at a funereal pace, bent over and shaking gourd and turtleback rattles. All the masks were different. Some resembled dogs with great teeth in elongated jaws. Others might have been eagles or hawks with enormous beaks and the ears of mules. The dancers' bodies were painted white or black or yellow and decorated with stylized lightning bolts, cornstalks, eagles, raindrops, and other symbols that Quill could not make out.

Two little girls dressed in white followed the dancers, one carrying a cross and the other the image of the Virgin Mary that seemed to be a staple of such processions. Behind the children came a double column of young women wrapped in shawls with pots balanced on their heads. They moved slowly, regally, frozen-faced, step-hesitation-step. Beneath their shawls, turquoise-set silver necklaces came fleetingly into view.

The missionary had found his way back to the rooftop. "SATAN COMETH! BEWARE!"

As his warning rang out, a fearsome figure swooped into the plaza, flapping wings of eagle and wild turkey feathers, which were bound to his bare arms by braided leather thongs. Little children hid behind their mothers. Lina Lituka moved through the crowd to stand beside Jane.

"My man," she said. "Rain Priest of the North."

The Rain Priest darted from one side of the plaza to the other, his importance manifest in a huge mask covered with black-and-white skunk skins, with the fur greased and clumped to stand out like nails. Black-and-white rings encircled a cylindrical long nose from which porcupine quills drooped. His bare torso was covered with white clay and daubed with green paint. Lightning streaked down his bare legs, which were gartered with tiny bells. Bells also tinkled along the bottom fringe of his kilt. In one hand he carried a gourd rattle, in the other a clay canteen shaped like a nursing woman's breast, its extended nipple the canteen's mouth. Ahead of him other dancers poked sharp-pointed planting sticks into the plaza floor and gestured as though pushing seeds into the ground.

The Rain Priest tipped his canteen to pour invisible streams of water over the symbolic seeds. At the site of the well he took a steel-tipped staff and drove it into the ground. A row of maidens lined up in front and behind him, stepping in place. Dancers circled around him, bells tinkling and shaking their rattles, while drummers kept up a steady beat. Standing tall, the Rain Priest began a sonorous chant.

"What's he saying?" Jane asked in a whisper.

"He ask earth gods to give us water and not blame us for what white men do," Lina whispered back.

Ninsulka abruptly stopped. The maidens took the pots from their heads, dipped hands into them, and danced past the Rain Priest, scattering cornmeal over the earth where the point of his staff rested.

"EVIL! Oh, EVIL!" cried the missionary from the rooftop.

* * *

A different kind of ceremony hailed the completion of the well. The sun was high and bright as a large crowd gathered around the brick wellhead. Many of the women bore empty pots on their heads in anticipation of being able to fill them. With Rain Priest Ninsulka standing at one side in everyday dress, Governor Kenoti held his ceremonial cane in one hand and with the other dipped a gourd into a shiny tin bucket of water cranked from the well's depths by Lina Lituka. Lifting the gourd to his lips, the governor drank deeply. He smacked his lips noisily and nodded his head.

"A-yah, a-yah," he said and dipped the gourd in the bucket again. He smiled in his usual tight-lipped way.

A boy of four or five stood near him, big-eyed and curious. Kenoti poured a dipper of water over the boy's head.

The crowd laughed as the boy ran dripping to his mother. Kenoti laughed with the rest, mouth open, teeth showing. His smile crinkled around the eyes. It looked genuine to Quill.

Everyone pressed forward to take turns sipping water out of the gourd.

Jane said, "Not very sanitary."

"Better than the river," Quill said.

Standing beside Quill, Sam Taylor said, "You done a good thing for these folks. If you ain't careful, before long they'll have you out there with a skunk mask on your head, flapping your wings."

Boys vied for a chance to crank up water to pour into the pots of waiting women. A scuffle broke out at the back of the crowd.

The missionary shouted, "Take your hands off me. I'm here to drive SATAN from this well and seek THE BLESSINGS OF GOD on the water He has so GRACIOUSLY brought us."

A group of mudheads surrounded him, gradually forcing him back along a passageway.

"O GOD, STRIKE DOWN THY ENEMIES!"

"Folks is getting edgy," the trader said. "There's more and more talk of the missionary being a witch. They blame him for the drought, and they're afraid he'll dry up the new wells like he done the springs. One of these days that saintly son of a bitch is going to give us all one hell of a headache."

* * *

On the last day of school, little girls danced around a maypole.

Boys lined up for stick races, in which each barefooted participant kicked a small piece of wood ahead of him as he ran. Some picked up the wood with their toes—no easy trick—and tried to run with it. At one side of the playground sheep roasted in fire pits and beans boiled in washtubs over open fires. Children and their parents passed along tables stacked with meat, beans, and bread to load tin plates. In the smoke and confusion Mrs. Wallis came to Quill, who was wearing an apron and dishing beans.

"Well," she said, peering at him from under the floppy brim of an enormous hat. "Well, so you've done it."

"Done what, Mrs. Wallis?"

"Got rid of me."

"I'm not sure what you're saying. Would you care for some beans?"

"Of course you know. I've been transferred to the Navajo reservation, to a place called Cornfields."

Quill dropped his ladle and took Mrs. Wallis aside.

"I hope you're pleased with yourself," she said.

"I didn't know that you had reapplied for transfer. The request didn't come across my desk."

"I didn't reapply. I was told to wait until an appropriate time, and I was never told when that would be. And then this, out of the blue."

"This is all news to me, Mrs. Wallis."

"Welcome news, I'm sure."

"As I hope it is for you, too."

"I do not appreciate being shunted aside in this arbitrary fashion, Mr. Thompson, and sent to a backwater I've never heard of. Cornfields!"

"You wanted to leave."

"Of course I wanted to leave. But I didn't expect to be

pushed out by your Washington friends without ceremony or notice."

"My Washington friends? I have no Washington friends."

"Don't lie to me, Mr. Thompson. That is the final insult, and I don't deserve it. To receive my orders in the mail from some nameless clerk, with no explanation—told to pick up and report to my new post immediately! How could you?"

"Mrs. Wallis, I assure you—"

She turned on her heel and marched off, firing one "Humph!" after another.

Chapter 18

Early one morning Sam Taylor drove into the school compound in a bright yellow Buick sedan. Its door panels and hood were trimmed in black, enhancing the brightness of the yellow. He had owned the car almost a year, replacing an ancient Packard, and it still didn't have five hundred miles on the odometer. He drove the Buick only on special occasions or when he just wanted to get away from the store and luxuriate behind the wheel for a little while with Flora beside him and the backseat stuffed with children. The trader was so proud of his Buick that every time he used it, even to drive no more than a mile or two, he and his little boys washed and polished it before he returned it to its place in the barn behind the trading post.

When he had to go to Gallup for supplies or on other business, which he did every few weeks, Taylor did not go in the Buick. Instead he used the old Packard, which he had converted from a battered sedan to a truck with dual rear wheels. He cut off the body behind the front seat and installed a wooden bed with stake sides that extended far beyond the rear wheels. To keep the front end from lifting off the road when the Packard was heavily loaded, he was careful to place most of the weight ahead of the wheels. Ramshackle as it looked, even in bad weather the noisy old vehicle could make in hours the trip from Gallup that took days for a mule train hauling supplies. The Packard was unlicensed now and lacked a muffler, but Taylor didn't worry about being stopped by the Gallup police.

"Cops that don't investigate but one murder in ten," he said, "ain't going to worry about a little thing like a license plate."

He based his dictum on the erroneous belief that most violent crimes occurred in the parts of Gallup known disparagingly by names such as Bohunkville and Little Mexico, where coal miners lived with their families in company houses and where the police rarely dared venture. In fact, what kept the cops busy were the fights, robberies, and murders that took place on and around Railroad Avenue.

When Taylor drove into the school compound in his Buick, Governor Kenoti and Rain Priest Ninsulka sat stiff as manikins on the edge of the backseat. Kenoti's trademark smile was pasted on his face, but Ninsulka lacked his usual sleepy look. Riding in an automobile was not an everyday thing. They were dressed much as they had been when Quill first met them—white trousers, velveteen tunics, and deerskin moccasins closed with silver buttons. The governor held his long wooden cane between his knees. The Spanish cross dangled from his neck.

Alone in the front seat, the trader looked like the chauffeur for a couple of oil-rich Osages from Oklahoma, a misimpression aided by the fact that he got out to hold the door for his passengers. By Awahi standards he, too, was formally dressed: pressed slacks, white collarless shirt, cloth cap, and well-shined black high-top shoes. It was his Buick-driving outfit.

"The governor and Ninsulka got a problem," Taylor said.

"So I figured, soon as I saw the Buick," Quill said.

He held the office door for them and gestured them through the gate to chairs in the fenced-off area where his desk stood. He offered cigarettes. The governor and Rain Priest each took two.

The trader pulled out his sack of Bull Durham and rolled his own. They all lit up and smoked in silence, covering the floor with ash, bluing the air. When Quill offered his cigarette pack a second time, Ninsulka and Kenoti again took two cigarettes each. Sam Taylor again rolled his own.

"And so," Quill said. "What do we have?"

"You know Hawalanee is the Sacred Mountain?" Taylor said.

"Of course."

"It's got shrines all over it. Shrines for every god you ever heard of, and more that you haven't. Some of them shrines go back before the Spanish, no one knows how far back. And there's caves, secret caves. Shrines and caves, all filled with ceremonial stuff, like ten-foot stilts and kachina costumes twice as high as any man. There's pots and fetishes and lots of other stuff. Most of it is real sacred. And there's Spanish armor they took off the conquistadores they killed in the rebellion of 1680. Ever since then they been tipping arrows and spears with that good Spanish steel. There's plenty of it left, still getting used. Lot of old graves up there, too, from all the times Awahis holed up on the Sacred Mountain to get away from enemies down below. You know how them old burials is. Necklaces, rings, bracelets, ceremonial masks, pots, all buried for the dead folks to use in the next world or wherever."

Taylor fell silent and rolled another cigarette, taking his time.

"And so?"

"So lately somebody's been working up there, grabbing anything they can get, including ceremonial stuff, sacred stuff."

"How long has this been going on?"

Taylor looked at the two Awahi men. The governor shrugged, as did Ninsulka. With occasional comments in Awahi tossed out by the two, Taylor then explained that ordinary

Awahis did not approach the mountain except in the course of fulfilling religious duties, such as when young boys went there for a three-day fast, seeking a name-giving vision before being initiated into manhood. Many of the sites might not be visited for years at a time, until some ceremonial need arose, and then the visit involved elaborate dances and chants to mollify the gods whose mountain it was and who did not like being bothered.

The first disturbed burial site had been spotted about a year earlier. But it appeared that it might have been the work of a bear, of which there were many on the Sacred Mountain. Since then, several more burial sites had been disturbed, and it had become clear that the intruder was human. Now the matter was growing more serious. A while back the elders had decided the village needed more Spanish steel to pound out for arrowheads. A steel-tipped arrow could kill a deer that a flint arrowhead, however well chipped and shaped, might not. One helmet or breastplate, laboriously flattened and hammered into thin sheets, would supply enough steel to fill the pueblo's needs for a generation or more.

To get the needed steel required two trips to the cave by a procession of dancers led by Ninsulka and dressed as kachinas. The first trip was to petition the gods for permission to enter the shrine. The second was delayed a few days to give the gods time to consider the request. If the petitioners could reach the cave on a second trip, it was clear to all that the gods approved. But when Ninsulka and his dancers made the second pilgrimage to the cave where the Spanish armor had been secreted for centuries, they found that its entrance had been breached in the interval. They had no full inventory of what had been in the cave, but they believed that at least two helmets and a breastplate were missing.

"That was a couple of weeks back," Taylor said, rolling

himself another cigarette. "Ninsulka, he set some of his Rain Society candidates to watching the mesa. Early this morning the boys seen somebody coming off the mesa, big burlap sack slung on his back, bulging with stuff."

"They recognize him? Who was it?"

Taylor seemed to ignore the question. "Fella, he hid the sack under them stacked boulders at the base of the mesa that we call Mother Rock. Looks like a big fat lady with three little kids tagging after her."

"I know the one you mean," Quill said.

"Then the fella, he come on back to Awahi, reading his Bible as he come."

"You're telling me it was the missionary?"

"That's right."

"And what did they do, the governor and Rain Priest?"

"They come to me and we drove to Hawalanee through the brush in my old Packard. All we found was a burlap sack filled with rocks. I reckon the missionary knew he was being watched and was thumbing his nose at Ninsulka and his boys. But Ninsulka and the governor, they say the word in the pueblo is that the missionary cast a spell on the stuff he took, so it turned into rocks when the sack was opened. And while we was up there at Mother Rock the thieving son of a bitch catches him a ride to Gallup with the trucker who delivered you a load of coal yesterday."

When last seen, the trader added, the missionary was tossing a suitcase, a couple of boxes, and several burlap sacks into the back end of the coal truck.

* * *

The weather was good and the road dry. They reached Gallup in just three hours in Quill's Model T—the best time Quill had ever made, though Governor Kenoti, Rain Priest Ninsulka, and the trader had to get out and push the car over the crest of a couple of steep hills. Sam Taylor's Buick might have made the trip faster, but Sam wouldn't subject it to the punishment. In Gallup they headed first to Parson's Grocery on the west edge of town. Quill and the trader went inside, leaving the governor and Ninsulka perched on the Model T's backseat.

"Friend of mine, Parsons is," Sam Taylor said. "Honest, and knows who's doing what. A gossip, you might say."

"I know him, buy my gas from him," Quill said.

Jim Parsons listened carefully to Sam's account of shrine-robbing at Awahi, pursing his lips and tapping a finger on the sharp tip of his long nose. When Taylor fell silent, Parsons nodded and brought his hand down from his face. He placed it palm-down on the worn linoleum covering his counter.

"Was I you," he said, "I'd talk to Honest John Holcomb there on Railroad Avenue. He's been getting plenty of good old stuff, burial stuff and the like, or so folks say. He don't say it's Awahi, though. Says he bought it from some Mexicans at Old Town when he was up to Albuquerque a week or so ago. Says he thinks it's Laguna or Acoma, maybe Zuñi, but don't know for sure."

"Have you seen the stuff?" Quill asked.

"Some of it, maybe not all. Honest John brought some by for me to look at, but the prices he was asking was too rich for my blood."

"What kind of things did he have?"

"Pots, mostly, but some prayer sticks, dance gourds, costumes. A Spanish helmet and a piece of armor, a breastplate, maybe."

"But you didn't buy any of it?"

"Just one little piece of silverwork that caught my eye. It

ain't Indian, though. Looks more Spanish to me. Honest John didn't know what it was, no more than me, but I offered him a dollar for it, and he bit."

Parsons opened his curio counter, unlocking it, and brought out a small silver object about two inches long. At one end it was rounded and pointed, like a toothpick; the other end was shaped like a tiny spoon. The center portion was flattened and elaborately carved on both sides with tiny cherubs and crucifixes.

Quill and Taylor took the object out to the Ford. The governor grabbed it and then passed it to Ninsulka, both talking at once.

"They say it was with the Spanish stuff stored on Hawalanee," Taylor said.

"Ask them what it is."

The governor poked it at his teeth, saying nothing.

"It really is a toothpick?"

"Looks like it," Taylor said. "But why the spoon?"

The governor turned the object around and dug in his ear.

"Ah," Taylor said.

Quill paid Parsons two dollars for the toothpick-ear spoon and bought gas, as well as longhorn cheese, a can of Vienna sausages, a box of gingersnaps, and two bottles of orange pop. There was no restaurant in Gallup that would serve the governor and Ninsulka. Nor were there any restrooms that they would be permitted to use, and Indians caught urinating in the alleyways were routinely given thirty days in jail at hard labor. Before cranking up the T-Model and driving into the center of town, Quill asked Parsons if his Awahi passengers could use his facilities.

"The old privy outside, sure," he said. "Can't nobody object to that."

Taylor suggested that he go alone to visit Honest John. "He see you with me, he'll pretend he don't know nothing about nothing."

Quill found a tree to park under, giving the governor and Rain Priest some shade while they ate lunch. The trader went to visit Honest John's Pawn and Curio Shop on Railroad Avenue and then to the Gallup Mercantile Co. to order supplies. Quill walked to the Piggly Wiggly on Coal Avenue to stock up on groceries. A trip to Gallup was a rare enough event that it couldn't be wasted. He had things to buy at a couple of other stores as well.

When Quill left on his errands, the governor and Ninsulka were sitting in the backseat of the Model T, munching cheese and sipping orange pop. When he returned a couple of hours later the two were nowhere to be seen. Sam Taylor was dozing in the front seat, his Stetson covering his face. He roused himself when Quill got in.

"Where'd the governor and Ninsulka get to?"

"They seen a couple of fellas from Zuñi, friends of theirs, who've been hired to put on dances for tourists at the El Navaho every night this week. They decided to stay over and see what it's like. May be a chance for some Awahi dancers to make a little money."

"How are they getting home?"

"Richard'll bring the truck up tomorrow to get the supplies I ordered at the Gallup Merc. He'll pick up Kenoti and Ninsulka, too."

"Any luck with Honest John?"

"Nope. Didn't really expect it. Claims he bought the stuff at Old Town, like he told Parsons. I didn't get to see it. He says a tourist come through this morning, California plates on his car, and bought the whole lot. Lying through his teeth, of course."

* * *

Before leaving Gallup, Quill drove to the McKinley County Courthouse to see the sheriff, though Sam Taylor predicted that nothing would come of it.

"We ain't going to find much interest there," he said.

The sheriff's office was in the basement of a courthouse wing that served as a jail and smelled of disinfectants. The sheriff wasn't in. A round-faced, rosy-cheeked deputy with tiny black eyes and up-tilted nostrils rimmed with black hair sat at a desk at the far end of the room, in front of a barred door leading to a corridor of holding cells. Long-term prisoners were housed on an upper floor.

As they went through the door, Sam Taylor said out of the corner of his mouth, "I know this bird. Hell, I've knowed better looking pigs than him. Smarter ones, too." To the deputy he sketched out their reason for coming to the sheriff. "We've had grave robbers at Awahi, old ceremonial pots and such-like. We heard they was seen here in Gallup."

The deputy opened a drawer and pulled out a daybook. With the stub of a pencil, he drew a line under the last entry on the page. He put the date and had them spell out their names.

"Quill?" he said. "That's a new one on me."

"It's from McQuillian, my mother's family."

"McQuillian? Then you wasn't giving me your true name?" The deputy put down his pencil stub and stared hard at Quill.

"I didn't suppose you needed my full name."

"You know, Mr.— ah, Mr. Thompson, I don't think you realize, this here's a serious matter. You come here and accuse somebody of a crime—"

"We're not accusing anyone. We're here to report a possible crime and ask for an investigation."

"This crime happened at Awahi? You know we ain't got jurisdiction on no reservation."

"But if the stolen goods are here in Gallup?"

The deputy fiddled with his pencil stub, turning it end over end, but not putting it to paper. "Ain't no crime to have curios here in Gallup."

The trader said, "But if it's stolen?"

"How we going to prove that? And besides, who cares? It's most likely just junk laying around on the ground, there for the picking up. If somebody'll pay good money for it, why not?"

"This stuff wasn't just laying around. It was taken from sacred shrines," Taylor said, his voice rising.

The deputy shook his head, cheeks redder than ever. "Sam, who cares? Don't rock the boat."

It was dark before they got home. As they neared Awahi, the ruts ahead of them were paved over with mouselike little creatures that Sam Taylor called kangaroo rats. The sudden beam of the Model T's headlamps seemed to mesmerize them. They stopped where they were, sat on their haunches, lifted their front paws, and turned their heads toward the lights until the car's wheels crushed them.

* * *

Jane was in the pueblo late the next afternoon when Richard squeezed the trader's Packard truck along the pueblo's narrow passageways. The governor and Ninsulka, their usually neatly coiffed hair windblown and their white trousers wrinkled and soiled, dropped off the truck as Richard stopped in the plaza. Both men looked as though they'd had little sleep.

A crowd formed instantly and helped unload a half-dozen or more burlap sacks from the back of the truck. Jane could not see the contents of any bag, but all were handled carefully, almost reverently.

When Jane reported what she had seen, Quill said, "I've a pretty good idea what was in those sacks."

"So have I," Jane said. "What are you going to do about it?"

"Nothing. I haven't reported the loss of the artifacts to Fort Frazier, and I won't report their recovery. The two crimes cancel one another out, and I can't prove either. Nor can anyone else. But I wouldn't want to be in the missionary's shoes here in Awahi."

Quill asked Sam Taylor whether Awahi dancers would be dancing for Fred Harvey in Gallup.

"Not that I know of," the trader said. "Why?"

* * *

The Gallup *Independent* reported:

> MYSTERIOUS BURGLARY
> AT HONEST JOHN'S
>
> During the early hours of yesterday morning, burglars broke into Honest John's Pawn and Curio Shop on Railroad Avenue and made off with several burlap sacks containing valuable Indian artifacts that the shop's owner, John Holcomb, purchased last week from the stock of an Albuquerque dealer who was going out of business. The artifacts, including pots, jewelry and several old dance costumes, were said to be from Acoma and Taos. Honest John said he paid more than $1,000 for the lot and has signed receipts to prove it. The loss is insured.
>
> Anyone having information about Honest John's loss is asked to contact Chief of Police Danny (Boots) Conner.

Chapter 19

In midsummer Quill and Jane spent a week at Santa Fe attending an annual conference of Indian Service teachers and medical personnel. On the first afternoon they attended a social mixer with fruit punch and cookies on the lawn in a sun-dappled grove of old elm trees outside the school's pueblo-style adobe dining hall. Mrs. Wallis pushed her way through the crowd to where Quill and Jane were standing. It was the first time they had seen her since the morning she left Awahi for Cornfields on the Navajo reservation.

She nodded dismissively at Jane and said to Quill without preamble, "I suppose you're still congratulating yourself."

"Hello, Mrs. Wallis," Quill said. "Why would I be doing that?"

"Why, on getting me out of your way, of course." She said it loudly, so all could hear.

"I'm afraid I can't claim credit for that."

"Humph! Lying as usual," she said, turning away.

The superintendent of the Shiprock District, whose jurisdiction included Mrs. Wallis's new post at Cornfields, was standing nearby.

"How did you do it?" the superintendent demanded. "Get rid of her at Awahi, I mean."

A few minutes later Quill encountered Mr. Thornton, who did not recognize him.

Quill introduced himself.

"Mr. Thompson? Do I know you?"

"I'm the principal at Awahi, sir."

"Awahi, you say?" Mr. Thornton looked Quill over, frowning slightly. "Haven't heard a thing about Awahi lately. Keep up the good work, Mr. Thomas."

* * *

When they got back from Santa Fe they found a paper sack hanging on the front doorknob. In it was a note—"ITS A GIRL"—from Sam Taylor, along with a cigar.

They went to the trading post without putting away groceries. Jane went directly to the house. Flora was up and about, days before Jane would have advised it, but no worse for it. The baby was plump, healthy, feeding well, and obviously full-term. She had been named Jane.

In the post Quill put his cigar in his shirt pocket to smoke later. Sam Taylor rolled his usual Bull Durham cigarette.

"Never was one for cigars," Sam said.

He soon took Quill over to meet the baby, though there were several Awahi customers in the bullpen and Richard was not around.

"You're not locking up?" Quill asked.

"What for?"

* * *

Richard Lituka's one-lung motorcycle skidded to a stop with dust billowing. Lina rode sidesaddle on the platform behind him. Quill and Jane went out to meet them.

Lina called, "Come quick. Miz Housma got trouble."

Before she could say more, Richard spun the putt-putt around and headed toward the bridge.

"I'll get my kit," Jane said. She made a point of taking it with her when she went out in the village. Quill cranked the Ford and was in the driver's seat by the time she returned.

"What do you think is going on?" Quill asked. He drove over the bridge faster than usual, making loose boards bang under the Model T.

"She's pregnant again," Jane said, "but the last time I saw her she was doing all right."

"You know her?"

"Not well. I've seen her several times professionally."

"You've never said anything."

"She asked me not to. She's a frightened woman."

"Frightened? Of what?

"That husband of hers."

Catching up with Richard, they followed him on a riverbank trail that skirted the waffle gardens, eagle pens, and corrals. They passed the missionary's Church of Jehovah's Sweet Light of Jesus Mission and followed the curve of the river a short distance to Reverend Housma's Reformed Church of the New Beginning Mission. It covered several acres and was surrounded by a barbed-wire fence on which the wind had plastered dried tumbleweeds. Within the fence stood a small frame building topped by a steeple. It had bars on the windows, a roof of red and gray shingles patched with tar paper, and two unpainted privies in back with doors sagging half open on leather hinges. This structure was both church and school. It had a dusty playground in front with two swings, a small baseball diamond, and a basketball backboard with a rusty hoop but no net. Like those at the government school, the swings blew back and forth in the wind as though unseen children were taking a turn.

Also within the barbed-wire fence, well away from the school and encircled by a second fence, this one of chicken wire, sprawled a large frame cottage. It had bars on its windows and a patchwork roof that matched the school's. In a field at the rear of the property, near a log corral and a ramshackle barn, two black-and-white cows—"Holsteins," Quill said—turned their tails to the wind. The barn's open doors revealed that it doubled as a garage for a new Essex automobile.

Quill stopped in front of the bungalow, leaving the motor running. Richard and Lina were waiting.

"Slut! Whore!" Housma was not in sight but Quill recognized his voice.

"Where is he?"

"In back," Richard croaked.

"Lord, help your faithful servant," Housma shouted. "Call down your lightning on this faithless wife and her paramour. Strike her dead, O Lord. Let her burn in Hell for her sins, now and forever. Amen."

Lina said, "Reverend Housma, he think missionary inside with Miz Housma."

"Has he been here? The missionary?" Quill asked.

"Not since she a little girl," Lina said. "But he don't believe that."

"What set him off?"

"Helen, she the housekeeper, she say Reverend rush into house, yell he see a man run across the field with cows. He grab belt. Yell some more. Miz Housma, she run to her room and lock door, won't open it. He go outside, try to look in window. He yell he see missionary in there. But the missionary, he still in Gallup. Nobody been here. Not today. Not any day. But Reverend, he think missionary always around. Helen, she sleep here. She say when Reverend and Miz go to bed, he watch Miz take clothes off. He yell, 'Where he touch you? Show me where he touch.' She beg and cry. She say he not been here, didn't touch her—not since she a girl. He take the belt. Whack, whack, whack. Then he fuck her. Reverend Housma not nice man. He my husband, I put his clothes outside the door, say bye-bye."

Quill went to the back and took a cautious look around the corner. Housma, hatless but buttoned up in his black suit, paced back and forth outside a heavily barred window. The bars ran across the window as well as up and down, forming small squares. He beat the ground with a long black belt. Each time its brass buckle struck the ground it kicked up a puff of dust.

"Sandringham, I swear to Almighty God, I'll kill you." Housma tilted his face Heavenward. His bald skull gleamed in the setting sun.

"Where are the children?" Jane asked.

"The kitchen," Lina said.

"Jane, you and Lina get them out, Mrs. Housma, too, and take them to our house," Quill said. "Richard, could you back me up?"

Richard nodded.

Jane hustled Mrs. Housma and three little boys out the door and into the car. Lina followed carrying a laughing toddler wrapped in a pink blanket. The Ford clattered off with Jane at the wheel, stretching to reach the pedals.

Quill stepped around the corner just as Housma rushed the house, shouting, "I'm coming in. The wrath of God shall smite thee down!"

He swung his belt at the window. The buckle bounced off the bars and hit the ground.

"Reverend Housma!"

Quill had to shout his name twice more before the man whirled to face him. When he saw Quill he fell to his knees. He shook his head as though shaking off raindrops.

"Brother Thompson!" he said, holding the belt behind his back out of sight. "I didn't realize you were here. Welcome. Join me in prayer, Brother. There is no better place to pray to the Lord than in His great open spaces, except of course in the sanctified environs of His house."

"I heard you have a domestic problem," Quill said. "Perhaps we should discuss it."

"Domestic problem? No. No. There can be no problem in a well-ordered household where the Lord reigns." He held out his free hand, palm open. The other hand remained out of sight behind his back. "On your knees, Brother Thompson, before the Lord! Join your hand with mine and ask forgiveness for your sins."

"Some other time, Reverend," Quill said.

He left the man on his knees and rode home on the back of Richard's putt-putt.

* * *

The three little boys sat on the top step of the Thompson's house, elbows on knees, chins on hands. The eldest child's eyes blazed with the blue green flame of an over-coaled fire. The two younger boys had the slate blue eyes of Reverend Housma.

"You boys ought to be inside, out of the wind," Quill said.

"Papa told us, never go in anybody's house," the boy with the missionary's eyes said.

"Your mother's inside. Wouldn't you like to be with her?"

"Papa wouldn't like it."

"At least come around to the side porch out of the wind."

"We'll stay here till Papa comes."

Inside Quill met Jane coming down the hall with a tray. On it was a half-empty teacup and a half-eaten piece of toast.

"How is she?"

"Scared out of her wits. I got her to lie down, but she's worried about her boys. I couldn't get them to come inside."

"Neither could I."

"She's covered with bruises but insists she's just awkward, always bumping into things. She's determined to go home as soon as she rests a few minutes."

They heard a car out front.

"That's Housma," Quill said.

"Send him away," Jane said. "We can't let him take her."

"But we can't stop her from going, either."

Mrs. Housma reached the hall before Quill got there. It was the first time he had seen her up close. She looked very young, with enormous deep blue eyes and wisps of blonde hair loose around her face. The ankle-length wrapper she wore barely closed over a bulging belly. Quill saw bruises on her face and arms.

"Stay in here," he said. "I'll talk to him."

"Please don't," she said. "I don't want him to hurt my boys."

Her little girl came out of the kitchen, holding one of Lina's fingers and dragging her pink blanket. She ran to her mother, who lifted her and staggered out into the wind. Mrs. Housma loaded the little boys into the backseat of her husband's new Essex and got in beside him with her daughter.

Quill said, "Well, we've been reminded of one thing."

"What?" Jane asked. "That Reverend Housma is as dangerous as he is hypocritical?"

"That at Awahi there's an eye behind every keyhole and an ear against every wall."

* * *

Days later the missionary reappeared at Awahi to harvest the alms-bearing letters that had arrived during his absence. He came as a passenger on a lumberyard truck laden with building supplies, which were soon stacked near the chapel of the Church of Jehovah's Sweet Light of Jesus Mission, USA, Inc. Word spread through the pueblo that the missionary was going to build a big new church and would need thousands of adobe bricks. He was hiring farmers whose crops were dying in the fields to mix clay and straw for the bricks and build the forms to shape them. For each adobe brick produced each day, he put a penny in a pot to be divided among those who had worked that day.

Lina Lituka told Quill that the missionary had taken over one of the new wells and was forbidding villagers to draw water from it.

"He say well is God's well. He say God needs all the water to make adobe for new church," Lina reported.

"We'll see about that," Quill said. "God didn't ask me."

He put on goggles to protect his eyes from the dirt-laden wind, jammed a broad-brimmed old Stetson on his head to keep off the sun, and jumped on the balloon-tired bicycle he had bought—Jane also had one—to navigate the sandy roads and paths around Awahi. He walked the bike across the rickety bridge and then rode along the river past the waffle gardens to the Sweet Light of Jesus mission. The road was just a trail through rabbit brush and greasewood, but busy. Every so often he had to stop to let an oncoming burro go past—he had quickly learned that the beasts tended to regard his bicycle as an excuse to kick up their heels and run away with their riders. The schoolchildren he met waved and smiled.

"'Ello, Misser Thoms," they called.

What pleased him even more was that the women he met no longer pulled their shawls over their faces and averted their eyes as he passed. He felt that he had become—or at least was becoming—an accepted member of the Awahi community. Not a friend, not a part of the village, but accepted in a friendly way—trusted. To his own surprise, he realized he felt at home.

The well was outside the pueblo and only a hundred feet or so from the missionary's property. It had been roped off and a crude sign posted:

GODS WELL
NO TRESPASING

Under a sunshade—an open framework of cottonwood logs covered with dried brush—the missionary sat cross-legged on the ground, his back to the wind, his bowler on his head, and his Bible open in his hand. A few steps in front of him, three Awahi men stirred clay into a long trench filled with water and clay. Other workers waited nearby in two lines, one line carrying buckets of water, the other buckets of clay. At one side stood a man holding an armful of straw.

The mixture of water and clay thickened. The missionary pointed at the water and clay bearers and at the straw man.

"You," he said. "You, you, and you. More water. More clay. More straw."

The first man dumped a bucketful of water into the trench and ran back toward the well. The second man emptied his bucket of clay. The third man darted forward and dropped in his sheaves. The stirrers slashed at the straw, mixing it in.

"Well, Reverend Sandringham, you've got quite a production line here," Quill said. He leaned his bicycle against his leg and pushed his goggles onto his forehead.

"Ah, Brother Thompson, it's good of you to come to see the progress we're making on Awahi's first truly worthy house of

God," the missionary said. "I know how busy your schedule is."

Quill dropped the "Gods Well" sign at the missionary's feet. "This is the people's well."

"You," the missionary called, pointing. "More clay. Quick now!"

"You're free to use all the water you need from your own well, Reverend Sandringham, but I am here to tell you that you are not to use another drop from a village well. That is an order. Do you understand?"

The missionary stood up, brushing dust off his trousers. He stepped over the "Gods Well" sign at his feet.

"I fear, Brother Thompson, that it is you who do not understand. When the Lord came to me, he said, 'BUILD MY HOUSE, YE GOOD AND FAITHFUL SERVANT.' 'I WILL, O Lord,' I said. And I promised Him four double rows of pews."

"Reverend Sandringham, I want you to listen carefully."

The missionary kept his eyes on the workers.

"It will be a beautiful structure," he said. "Small, of course—my congregation of God-loving, Bible-dedicated souls is not large, but growing—and it will have no adornment other than a simple cross. Plastered white, of course, inside and out."

"Reverend Sandringham, listen to me."

"The Lord pointed out to me that it would take years to make all the adobe bricks we will need for God's House using the primitive methods employed by these ignorant people. 'ORGANIZE,' He said. 'MAKE THEM WORK TOGETHER!' And that is what I have done. Instead of twenty or thirty bricks a day, I believe we'll soon be turning out ten times that number by using the Lord's far more efficient methods. MANAGEMENT, my dear sir. MANAGEMENT is what these people require."

"That's fine, Reverend, but I am telling you to use your own water for it."

The missionary turned his eyes full-force on Quill and for the first time seemed to take in what he was being told.

"My well is too shallow. It won't supply the Lord's needs. I HAVE NO CHOICE."

"Don't you know there is a drought? The four wells we have dug are also shallow, barely able to supply enough water to keep the people alive. Do you want them to suffer?"

"If that is God's will," the missionary said. "Suffering will bring them to the Lord, once His house is built. TRUST ME. I KNOW WHEREOF I SPEAK. I KNOW THE WILL OF GOD."

He turned back to the workers. "You," he cried. "More water!"

"Not another drop," Quill said.

He mounted his bicycle and rode off to post a guard at each well.

Chapter 20

At the trading post a few days later Sam Taylor said, "Big news. Kenoti give me a message for you. He says him and Ninsulka is calling a rabbit hunt. Wants to know if you want to join in."

"I thought outsiders weren't allowed in a rabbit hunt."

"They ain't. Guess he's telling you that you ain't no outsider no more. It's a big honor. Really surprised me. First government man I know to get an invite. In fact, up to now I been the only white ever took part in a rabbit hunt. Of course, being married like I am and all, I'm practically one of 'em."

"I used to shoot rabbits as a kid, back in Texas, dog years ago."

"This is different. No guns. Somebody get killed, was there guns. Besides, guns don't fit what this hunt is really about. They whack 'em with sticks all right, but killing rabbits is only part of it. Lots of religion in it. Their religion. Will you do it?"

Quill narrowed his eyes, thinking about issues of church and state. "Should I?"

"You damn well got to. Be an insult, not to. I'll show you the ropes."

On the day of the hunt Quill dressed, as the trader advised, to keep the sun, bugs, and snakes off: wide-brimmed hat, long-sleeved shirt, khaki pants, high-top shoes and leather leggings, with a canvas-covered army canteen looped over one shoulder.

He was waiting when Taylor crossed the bridge to the school just before sunrise in the old Packard he had converted into a truck. In the back of the truck two topless wooden barrels were full to the brim with water. A tin dipper hung from the top rim of each barrel. Richard rode facing backward at the rear of the truck bed, legs dangling, bracing himself against bumps with his arms, which thrust his shoulders up almost even with his ears.

They crossed the bridge and skirted the pueblo, bouncing along the rutted road. Quill grabbed the top of the windshield to keep his seat. With no top over him, no door beside him, he expected on every bump to be flipped out of the truck.

"After we drop off for the hunt Richard'll follow in the truck with the water," Sam said. "Going to be a scorcher. Folks'll welcome a drink now and again. So'll we."

"Richard won't be in the hunt?"

"Too much walking. Richard, he can do anything that don't make him bend much or raise his arms too high, but he don't like to walk far or fast."

Bent over the wheel, fighting to keep the truck in the ruts and all but yelling to make himself heard over the roar of the motor, Sam told Richard's story again. It was the second time Quill had heard the story, but this time the trader carried it further, telling what happened to the pueblo after Richard was whipped as a witch and left crippled.

As soon as John Purvis, the trader, heard that the Warrior Priesthood had seized Richard, he sent Sam Taylor to Fort Frazier, which by then was no longer an army outpost. The authorities there had a federal magistrate deputize the McKinley County sheriff and a posse of ranchers and Gallup businessmen as federal marshals, and dispatched them to put down what was regarded as an uprising. The sheriff and his men had only contempt for the

Awahis, and the ranchers among them coveted Awahi land. They treated the Awahis roughly, and when the Awahis fought back, the National Guard was called up and federalized. Two hundred heavily armed troops stormed the pueblo, killing two Awahi bowmen, as well as three women and an infant who happened to get in the way of Guard bullets. The Rain Priest of the North, the pueblo governor, and members of the tribal council were held in the Gallup jail while Washington decided what to do with them.

"It was a terrible time," Sam Taylor said.

The governor and the Rain Priest both died in jail. The sheriff claimed the two old men fought in their cell and beat one another to death. It was a story that no one in Gallup doubted and no one at Awahi believed. The other prisoners were eventually released for lack of evidence, because no Awahi would admit to knowing anything about anything.

After the deaths of the governor and Rain Priest, the land-hungry ranchers among the sheriff's posse went to court, arguing that the Awahis' resistance to the posse proved that the tribe was lawless and incompetent to manage its own land.

"Did the court go for that?" Quill asked.

"Oh, you bet," Taylor said. "The courts took over running the pueblo's affairs. Leased thousands of acres of grazing land to whites for pennies per acre, not knowing no better. There's still lawsuits going on over that. Someday the Awahis will get the land back. Hell is, though, them ranchers know they'll lose the land in the end, so they don't give a tinker's damn how they treat it. They put two, three times as many head on it as good sense says they should. By the time the land comes back to the Awahis, what they'll get is a lot of country that's been overgrazed for so long it'll be desert and won't do nobody no good."

The road petered out. Sam followed faint wagon tracks over

slickrock and through sand, sagebrush, and greasewood.

"Hunt's going to be up on Diablo Flats," he said.

Diablo Flats, at the base of Hawalanee, was one of Awahi's three principal outlying farming areas, where the men of the pueblo planted corn and wheat.

They lurched and bounced over the plain, with Sam driving straight ahead over sagebrush that banged and scraped the underside of the floorboards. Dust rose all around them, clogging their nostrils and stinging their eyes. Ahead Quill could see puffs of dust raised by the feet of Awahi men stripped to loincloths, trotting barefooted. In the slanting light of the newly risen sun, their heels dragged undulating shadows over clumps of sage. On their shoulders the runners carried curved pieces of wood that the trader called rabbit sticks. Bundles of clothing dangled from the sticks.

"Fellas run like that to and from the fields, every day—ten, twenty miles. It'd kill me," Sam said. "I can spit farther'n I can run, but these is tough folks, even the old farts like him. Don't faze 'em."

The runner lifted his stick in a salute as they passed.

"We could give him a ride," Quill suggested.

"Nope. If he asked, sure. But us to offer—that'd be a insult."

"Insult?"

"Yeah. He'd think we was saying he's too old to run anymore. Folks have pride."

There were more runners around them now, each with his rabbit stick and bundle, and wagons loaded with women dressed in their ceremonial best. Some gray heads, too old to run, plodded along or rode on donkeys.

Ahead of them, Quill caught the glint of a golden head. The missionary.

"Look at the son of a bitch," Sam said. "He don't give up. He come to me and asked could I get him a invite. I told him no. Ninsulka would've been sore as hell if I tried. So what does the missionary do? What you'd expect. Just pushes his way in."

"I thought he'd been pretty calm since we stopped him from stealing water," Quill said. "Haven't seen much of him. Or heard."

"You ain't been out in the village much then. Like always, he's been roaming around, shouting in people's ears, pulling magic tricks. Bad as he ever was. But he ain't done no more grave robbing, not that I know of. 'Course, Kenoti's boys is watching him like a hawk."

The Packard caught up with him. The missionary was loping along at a steady pace. He wore only an old pair of khaki pants, cut off above the knee, much too big for him and bulging around his hips—filled with magic props, Quill assumed. A rolled red bandanna kept his flowing hair out of his eyes. Sweat rolled down white shoulders, turning the thick reddish gold hair on his back into black whorls. He had a rabbit stick on his shoulder, but no dangling bundle.

The trader slowed the truck alongside. "You want water?" he shouted over the motor's roar.

The missionary did not pause. "Bless you, Brother Sam, but I have plenty."

A Mason jar appeared in one hand without a break in stride. Almost at once the jar disappeared and reappeared in the other hand, the hand that steadied the rabbit stick on his shoulder. Quill would have sworn that the hands had not come close to one another.

"You oughta have a hat." Sam lifted his own dusty black Stetson. "A shirt, too. You'll be sun-foozled afore long."

"The Lord is my shelter as well as my shepherd."

"Damn fool," Sam said, driving on. "Still, I ain't ever able to get as mad at him as I'd like. Son of a bitch did me a big favor, I was young."

He told Quill again about his youthful misadventures in Gallup's red-light district, but in the absence of Jane told it in greater and more lurid detail, and went on to retell the story of how the missionary had rescued him and made him a loan to replace the money he'd lost. He repaid the loan and his boss never learned of young Sam's misadventure.

"Never had a drink since and never wanted one," he said. "You could say the missionary done redeemed my life, though I managed to keep him off my soul, if I have one."

"How come he had the money to lend you?" Quill asked.

"Dunno. He never said and I never asked. Probably cards. He may be a missionary, but he's one hell of a card shark, too. Not to mention boozer and cocksman."

"Maybe he was the one who took the money out of your pockets?"

"Could be, I reckon, but it don't signify. However he got the money to loan me, he pulled me out of a hell of a hole. If it was him, though, I wish he hadn't took my good-luck piece, too." He told Quill again about the 1883 silver dollar with the copper loop soldered on the back.

"Ask him sometime?" Quill suggested.

"Can't do that. Wouldn't be grateful."

The Packard detoured around a prairie-dog town, jounced slantwise down the steep banks of a couple of dry arroyos and back up again. Soon they came into the shadow of Hawalanee. The rising sun had not yet cleared the Sacred Mountain.

At one end of Hawalanee's mass, a couple of miles ahead over a boulder-strewn plain, Quill could see slender rock formations with vaguely human shapes.

"Them formations there is the Twins," Sam Taylor shouted. "Got their name, the Twins did, because a long time ago, longer than anyone remembers or knows, the gods got angry because they thought folks was neglecting them—just like now, it may be—and they decided to punish the people."

The trader told Quill how the gods made a great rain fall from the sky, day after day, never stopping. A flood swept through the valley, driving the people from the pueblo to higher ground, rising higher than the top of the highest houses and then higher than the highest hills. Soon the people were on the slopes of Hawalanee clambering up its rocky sides with the water rushing past just below their feet. Still the water rose. As they looked out over the valley all they could see was water. It was a vast sea and still rising. Finally the people reached the top of the Sacred Mountain, expecting to find safety in the abode of the gods and their eagle messengers. But the water kept rising.

The Rain Priest of the North announced that the gods had spoken to him. The anger of the gods was so great they could be appeased and the water stopped only by a monstrous human sacrifice. So a handsome boy and his twin sister, the comeliest girl of the village, were dressed in fine raiment and laden with jewelry. After many prayers the children were pushed into the raging waters, which by then were reaching the very top of Hawalanee. As soon as the boy and girl hit the water they turned to stone on the spot, the skies cleared, and the waters fell. Ever after, when Awahis looked toward Hawalanee they saw the Twins standing there and were reminded to pay proper homage to the gods.

Later, in another period of hard times, the gods spoke to another Rain Priest of the North, saying that once was enough. No more human sacrifices. A nice rabbit stew would please the Holy Ones just as much.

"And that's what this here rabbit hunt is all about," the trader said. "Folks figure times like this—drought, poor crops, talk of witches—mean the gods is sore as a boil again. Maybe it's time for a special rabbit stew to make 'em feel better."

"Might also get rid of some of the rabbits that are eating what crops there are," Quill said.

"Might, but that ain't the main point. Believe it or not."

They passed fields of stunted corn, each with its own crude scarecrow, most of which had one or more crows perched on it, and came to Diablo Flats. As they neared the Twins, they passed more and more runners, more and more wagons filled with women. They were in higher country now, and small junipers were interspersed with the sagebrush and greasewood. Ahead Quill saw smoke rising at the base of Hawalanee.

"Smoke there, that's the blessing fire," Sam shouted. "The kachinas, they been up there all night, chanting and dancing. Soon's everybody gets up there, or most of 'em, they'll spread out and get started."

The runners and wagons converged on the fire, a mound of burning junipers. Sam stopped the truck. He and Quill each drank a dipper of water from the barrels in the rear.

"Save your canteen for later," Sam advised.

He handed Quill a rabbit stick. It was flat and heavy, smooth as polished turquoise.

"Oak or ash, I think, or something like," Sam said, "an old one, don't know how old. I've got four of 'em. My father-in-law give me this one when his knees went bad on him."

"It looks sort of like a boomerang," Quill said.

"I reckon, but it don't come back to you. And you don't always throw it. If a rabbit comes by, just take a swing at it."

Quill swished the stick through the air, getting the feel of it.

Richard hobbled up from the back of the truck. Without speaking, he pulled himself up to the driver's seat, turned the truck around, and drove down the slope a short way. Several men, wearing the pants and shirts they had carried on their rabbit sticks, climbed up on the truck bed. Taking the dippers hanging on the barrels, they sipped water and handed the dippers around, laughing and talking.

Around the bonfire of burning trees, dancers with painted bodies stepped back and forth. They wore black and green masks with slits for eyes and mouths, white kilts, and knee-high deerskin boots. Three men sat on the ground, gently slapped hollowed-log drums that they held between their knees, and chanted softly, sometimes singly, sometimes in unison.

"They're telling the tribal story," Sam Taylor said.

"I can't catch a word," Quill said.

"Nobody can. They go lickety-split. There's a lot to tell."

The kachinas took turns going off a short distance one by one and publicly relieving themselves. Men around the truck took dippers of water to them. A dancer accepting a dipper turned his back to the fire, slipped off his mask, and drank, emptying whatever was left in the dipper over the top of his head, cooling off, before putting the mask on again and resuming his place in the ceremony.

To Quill the procedure seemed as casual as a country barn dance back home in Texas. He said so.

"That ain't it," Sam said. "It's all done one, two, three, nothing left out. This is serious business, and if it ain't done right, God knows what dirty trick the gods'll play next. That's how they feel about it."

A little girl wearing a green print dress that fell straight from her shoulders to her knees—a school dress—thrust a bowl filled with bits of bread at Quill. She looked familiar, but he did not know her name. She ducked her head, said nothing.

Sam Taylor said, "We're supposed to take a little bread and throw it in the fire. Feed the gods. Pass your stick through the fire, too. Gives you luck."

No one seemed to be in charge. With no signal that Quill was aware of, two hundred or more men and boys began to space themselves around an area that he estimated as covering ten acres or so. A vast circle formed, centering on the smoldering tree and stretching out over Diablo Flats. Women and girls stood outside the lines, prepared, the trader said, to act as gatherers.

Still with no evident signal, the circle began to tighten. Almost at once a jackrabbit was flushed from the upper slope, where Sam Taylor and Quill had found places. Its big ears plastered along its body almost to the tail, the rabbit dashed toward the perimeter, trying to escape. Nearby men, including Sam, threw their sticks. All missed, but the flying sticks coming from several directions confused the jack. It broke stride and whirled back, running across in front of Quill. He threw his stick, aiming just ahead of where the animal seemed to be headed. The stick curved through the air, seeming to float, seeming to take forever, and struck the rabbit's neck. To Quill's surprise the jack flopped on the ground, suddenly helpless.

"Got him!" Quill yelled. He raced over, picked up his stick, and waved it over his head.

"First one!" Sam whooped. All around men were shouting now, still trotting forward. For the moment, Quill again felt himself one of them.

A row of young girls who looked to be ten to twelve years old rushed through the line of hunters. The first to reach the dying rabbit was the girl in the green school dress. She picked it up by the ears and ran to the fire, where the masked kachinas were dancing.

Sam and Quill stopped to watch. One kachina plucked fur from the rabbit's tail and threw it into the fire. Another slit the animal's nose with his knife, making blood gush, as the girl, solemn-faced, lifted her skirt. The dancer rubbed the animal's bleeding nose down the inside of her thighs.

"This first rabbit is for the gods," the trader said. He explained that putting the little bit of fur in the fire was meant to thank the gods for good hunting. Smearing the blood on the girl's leg asked them to make her and all the young girls fertile when they became women.

"Tonight," Sam said, "there'll be a big ceremony over your rabbit, and then they'll throw him in a sacred fire for the gods to feast on. The rest of the rabbits we get today will get ate by the people—lot of full bellies tonight."

Quill and the trader turned to rejoin the circle of hunters. They heard a commotion behind them.

"SHAME! Oh, EVIL!"

Quill stopped, wiping his face with his arm. His shirt was soaked through, and he could feel sweat rolling down his legs.

Sam Taylor stopped, too. "What's the son of a bitch up to now? Don't he have no sense at all?"

The missionary had a grip on the girl whose legs had been bloodied. Hunters rushed to push him away and free the screaming child.

"You have defiled this child," the missionary shouted. "SHAME! SHAME! SHAME!"

"I better go sort this out before somebody gets hurt," Quill said.

"Let them handle him, the damned fool."

It took only a moment or two to subdue the missionary and free the girl. They hustled him out of the rabbit circle, past the ring of women who were darting in to pick up the jackrabbits as they were felled. Whenever the missionary tried to push his way forward, hunters lifted their rabbit sticks and forced him back. He raced back and forth in the blazing sun, waving his Bible and shouting. Quill could not tell what he said. The festive screaming as rabbits were flushed and killed drowned out his words.

By noon more circles had been formed and closed. Rabbit carcasses were stacked high on the wagons that accompanied the hunt. Quill and the trader found themselves near the Packard truck.

"I've had enough, if you have," Taylor said.

"More'n enough," Quill said, draining the last water from his canteen.

He and Sam waved Richard down and climbed into the back end of the truck, between the two water barrels, which were now empty. Already lying there was the missionary, lobster red and barely conscious.

"Sunstroke, I'd reckon," Sam said.

"We'd better get him home and let Jane have a look at him," Quill said.

"Goddam fool."

"Take not the name of the Lord in vain," the missionary muttered.

Chapter 21

The rabbit hunt did not bring rain. As summer ended, drought stunted the squash and melons in the women's waffle gardens. Clouds of grasshoppers devoured every green thing, from blades of grass to the green thread used in the embroidery on ceremonial kilts drying in the sun. Next came an infestation of corn borers to destroy much of the crop that had survived drought and hoppers. The harvest that year was the poorest in living memory. Storerooms that by then should have been bursting with good things were half filled, if that. Looking ahead, housewives reduced the size of the meals they served and prayed for an easy winter.

People spoke of witches and whispered names. Neighbors pointed to neighbors. Warrior Priesthood members searched any number of the medicine sacks possessed by Awahi men, looking for anything out of the ordinary—a dried bit of loco weed, for example, which might have the power to poison someone. In each medicine sack they seized, however, they found only what was expected: the dried umbilical cord of the sack's owner and a bit of fluffy down he had pulled from an eaglet on the cliffs of Hawalanee as he entered manhood.

Even Jane came under suspicion. The little girl who had taken the first rabbit to the gods stepped in a prairie-dog hole and broke her leg. It was a compound fracture and soon infected. Jane was not called in until the child's leg was the size of a fat woman's thigh. She cleaned the wound and set and splinted the leg, but there was little she could do. The child died. Villagers whispered: Miz Thoms had splinted the little girl's leg, hadn't she? The child had died, hadn't she? Could the principal's wife be the witch who was showering agony on Awahi?

But suspicion soon focused more sharply than ever on the missionary. During his long illness after the rabbit hunt—it took weeks for him to recover—his church-building enterprise languished. It became clear to more and more that the crazy white man was the witch responsible for the child's death. As doubts about him proliferated, parents rushed into the passageways to pull children out of his path as he brought forth balls from his ears and eggs from his mouth. His small congregation dwindled to a fervent few.

The missionary seemed not to notice. He wrapped his great cloak about him against an early cold spell and plunged through the pueblo, doing his tricks with chapped and cracking bare hands. However loudly he spoke, people turned their backs and did not listen. Undeterred, he tried to do his Bible-into-ball trick. The wind seized the ball and lifted it, a dot of green, into gray skies high over the stacked houses toward the Sacred Mountain. The missionary could not call it back.

People saw that as an omen, though of what was not clear.

* * *

When the drought finally broke, the moisture came as snow. A foot fell in mid-November and did not melt as one storm followed another. Sam Taylor said it was the longest, coldest, bleakest winter he could remember. The melt from the snowpack in the mountains would be welcome when spring came, but for now the snow only added to the misery of scant food and dwindling stocks of wood for Awahi fires. Haystacks dwindled and livestock was turned loose to graze but found few protected areas where grass was not covered by snow. Wind-driven snow blocked roads, cutting the pueblo off from the outside world. No one could come or go. There was no truck to bring mail or supplies for the school. Quill kept a worried eye on the dwindling stores of beans and mutton in his warehouse.

He found one benefit in the freezing weather: A lake that the drought had not emptied was frozen over. He hired Awahi men to cut ice and haul it on mule-drawn sledges to the school. For the first time Lina Lituka could remember the icehouse was full, with enough ice buried in sawdust to last a full school year. When there was no more room for ice Quill sent the ice cutters with their saws and sledges into the mountains for wood to replenish the pueblo's fast-dwindling supply of fuel.

That was an unauthorized use of government funds and equipment, and only a few months earlier Quill might have agonized over the decision. Now he acted without hesitation, contenting himself with making a full account of the transgression in the report he would send to Fort Frazier as soon as the road cleared.

* * *

Well before Christmas—"Kissmus," the children called it, already anticipating the candies and small gifts passed out by the government and mission schools—attendance dropped off, especially among older students. The decline surprised Quill. He had counted on the hot meal served at noon every day to keep the children in school, especially given the scant harvest that had halved the pueblo's usual winter stores. The more children he fed at the school, the longer the food supply in the village would last. Quill could not account for the decline in students eating lunch.

He consulted Sam Taylor at the AW HI DING COM trading post.

"Happens every year," the trader said. "Not much you can do about it. Whole pueblo is busy as can be getting ready for Klahiako."

"Klahiako?"

"That's the big harvest celebration. It's held around our Christmas time every year to thank the Klahiako gods for such a good harvest. Folks come from all over, even old enemies like Navajos and Mexicans, and they all got to be treated like big buddies and fed to the gills and let to wander anywheres they want to go—except the kivas, of course."

"But it wasn't a good harvest," Quill said. "Awahi doesn't have enough food stored to do much more than feed itself. People could be starving before the new crops come in."

"Maybe so," the trader said. "But that don't count." He paused to roll and light a cigarette, which bobbed in the corner of his mouth, the ash growing, as he talked. "Folks is looking ahead. They know bad times is coming, but they don't dare complain. If they did, the Klahiako would be offended, and the harvest next year mightn't be worth a tinker's damn. So belly up, boys, and help yourself—it's all free. Except the booze, of course."

"Booze? Bootleggers here at Awahi?"

"Can't keep them out. Most folks, the elders especially, don't like it, but there ain't much they can do about it. They ain't supposed to turn people away at Klahiako, and bootleggers is people, too. So the moonshiners pour in and set up their wagons down by the river, sell their rotgut on the sly, and stuff their bellies like they was honorable citizens from just down the street."

"I'd like to stop the bootlegging," Quill said.

"You'd need an army," Taylor said, "and you still couldn't do it without you get Kenoti and Ninsulka to back you. And that'll take time. You might could get 'em going next year or the year after, but it ain't going to be easy even with them and an army—and I can promise you, you won't have an army."

* * *

When Klahiako came, not even bootleggers could make their way to Awahi. Wind-driven snowdrifts blocked the roads and trails for the hordes of outsiders who usually appeared to feast on Awahi sheep, goats, and yearling calves roasted whole over glowing pit fires. Quill thought Awahi's temporary inaccessibility was just as well. The lack of foreign guests whose needs or demands could not be refused meant that the pueblo's depleted winter stores would last longer, easing the threat of starvation later on. Jane saw still another benefit in the weather-imposed isolation. Without visitors' germs, Awahi might be spared the epidemic of flu or measles that was the usual aftermath of mass intrusions.

The villagers did not share her satisfaction or Quill's. Hospitality, the sharing of good things with the gods and all others—this was what Klahiako was all about and what the gods demanded, privation and epidemics be damned. Every family would offer every guest who crossed their threshhold gifts and all the food they could eat, urging them to take more. When the Klahiako gods came in ghostlike ten-foot splendor across the river, Lina Lituka told Jane, one or another of the gods would visit every house in the pueblo before the night was over. They were too tall to enter any house but would bend to peer in a door or window as drums and flutes announced their presence. It might have been a poor harvest, but it was what the gods had provided, and they must be thanked as though it had been bountiful.

Without visitors to share with, the zest would go out of the celebration. To serve friends was pleasant, but to serve enemies as though they were one's brothers—*there* was a true test of character, an incontrovertible measure of devotion that was bound to please the gods and bring good fortune.

* * *

Quill and Jane huddled on the bridge with Lina Lituka, their backs to the screaming wind. Stars sparkled in the sky and the moon was full. Through chattering teeth Jane chanted a verse out of her West Texas childhood: "Clear as a bell, cold as hell, and the damnedest frost that ever fell."

Six Klahiako impersonators—six being a magic number for the Awahi—plodded toward the bridge along the dry riverbed, sheltered from the wind by the clifflike bank. Not yet in full regalia, the gods looked like ordinary beings wrapped in heavy blankets. They struggled through the snow surrounded by twenty or more near-nude mudheads. The clowns were blanketless and coatless, grotesque in clay masks, their bodies smeared with white clay. The lightning bolts and other symbols painted on their chests and backs, their legs and arms as well, seemed to glow with supernatural intensity in the moonlight. Some mudheads carried the costumes the gods would soon put on; others raced ahead, gesturing at the gods in an effort to step up the pace.

"Mudheads cold. They say, hurry up," Lina said from within a Pendleton blanket drawn over her head.

"I'm freezing, and I'm all bundled up," Jane said.

Quill put his arm around her and drew her closer. He stamped his feet on the boards of the bridge. "Me, too," he said.

The procession climbed the riverbank toward the bridge.

"Over the bridge. That how we do it now," Lina said. "Old days gods wade across river. Now go on bridge. My husband say young men lazy now. No guts, my husband say."

Jane tried to pull Lina closer.

"My blanket warm," Lina said, drawing away.

"When do the children first see the gods?"

"Klahiako put on costumes. Then wait. Children run out when gods climb up the bank like they come across river."

Lina turned her back on the procession as it shuffled past on the bridge. Quill and Jane followed suit, pretending to see and hear nothing.

On the other side, it all happened as Lina said it would. The mudheads helped the gods disappear into towering costumes that made them ten feet tall, with pointed heads, turkey-feather hair, enormous bulging eyes, and wide-open yellow beaks a foot long. They looked like giant birds, dangerous birds. Mudheads steadied them and their costumes against the wind.

The gods positioned themselves on a sloping path just below the rim of the steep riverbank. As children spilled out of the pueblo the gods came up over the edge. The mudheads tossed candy—donated, Lina said, by Sam Taylor—high into the air. The children slid over the frozen snow, chasing pieces of candy but trying to stay away from the gods, shrieking if they came close.

"Santa Claus just came," Quill said, "but he's scary."

"That all right," Lina said, sounding miffed. "Nothing wrong."

The missionary came rushing out of the passageway. "SAVAGES! HEATHENS!"

He spat at the Klahiako.

"EVIL! Oh, EVIL," he cried.

Mudheads tried to seize him. Evading them, he slipped and fell, sliding on his belly over the ice past the gods and through the children, heading like an unsteered sled down the slope toward the riverbank. Just short of the edge he stopped himself by grabbing a sagebrush sprig poking up through the snow and ice.

Mudheads were on him at once. They held him face down

in the snow, silencing him, until everyone else was inside the pueblo.

* * *

Quill and Jane followed Lina along passageways sheltered from the wind and through one plaza after another, where whole sheep were roasting on spits over glowing coals and other fires burned for warmth and light. They did not trail the Klahiako, who were mobbed with children hoping for and often getting more of the candy and small gifts tossed to them by the gods' mudhead escorts. Instead they struck off along other crowded alleys toward Lina's house. Everywhere the crowds were thick, and everywhere they met kachinas, singly and in groups, dressed in ceremonial costumes and masks. Some represented wolves, or eagles, or bears; others were unearthly. Some had a benign look, but others looked threatening.

In one small plaza Lina pointed out four particularly horrific kachinas filing past. Children shrank against the walls or tried to hide behind their mothers when this group passed, doing the traditional dance step. "Mialosota," Lina explained. "Not gods but strong. Sometime they look like one thing. Sometime something else. They find out who done bad thing just by sniffing. We tell Mialosota stories. Kids know the stories not true, but they scared anyway. When child do something wrong, parents say, 'Mialosota get you.' Kids hide."

"Like bugbears with us," Jane said.

These Mialosota had legs wrapped in shaggy gray wolf skins, with many tinkling small bells fastened to them. From old cartridge belts—army discards, Sam said—wrapped around their waists dangled more bells, along with knives, broken arrows, and the dried skins of small animals. Their torsos were painted white, with zigzag lightning bolts and many small balls of bloodred or bright yellow. Most hideous of all were their clay masks, which had white circles around the eyeholes and long wolves' snouts with hairy nostrils and green-lipped mouths. The mouths were open, showing enormous white teeth, spotted with red. Each mask was topped by what looked to be a small eagle with outspread wings and a sharp, gaping beak, outthrust as though about to tear someone's flesh.

The Mialosota carried brightly painted gourd rattles in one hand, coiled whips in the other. They pointed the whips menacingly at the cowering children and every so often one would single out a child and snap a whip at the terrified evildoer, the tip of the whip not quite reaching. Other children, no longer in danger of being targeted, laughed.

* * *

Quill had to bend low to get through the door of Lina's house and stayed bent once inside. Lina led them to seats on a ledge at the end of a crowded, smoky room near a dome-shaped fireplace where guests leaned over one another to toast morsels of food in the flames. On the hearth and the nearby floor were bowls and baskets heaped with breads of all kinds—flat breads, loaves, and twists wrapped around sticks and thrust into an open blaze—as well as vegetables, stews, mush, and meats of every variety in big open pots that were being constantly replenished. Everyone was eating, dipping fingers or bits of bread in the pots while the women of the house passed other pots around the room, urging more dishes on those they perceived to be slowing down. Everyone was talking and laughing. The sound level was so high that anyone who did not shout would not be heard.

"Ain't the same without no one from outside," Sam Taylor said, sitting down beside Jane. "Most years you'd have lots of Navajos mixing in, right at home, stuffing their bellies. 'Have more of this, friend.' 'Try this, honored visitor.' Fun to watch, folks treating enemies like they was kissin' cousins."

Sam's wife appeared in front of Jane. Like Lina and other women in the room, Flora wore ceremonial finery: a one-piece, knee-length black dress of finely woven wool with elaborate embroidery at the hem, draped over one shoulder and belted at the waist, worn over a long white slip, with white moccasins and leggings of soft deerskin, along with silver and turquoise necklaces and bracelets.

"Try this," she said, offering a stick with a blackened strip of something wrapped around the end. "Roasted rabbit."

It did not look appetizing, but Jane took the stick without hesitation.

"It's good," she said. "Kind of a cedar flavor."

Flora nodded. "The fire," she said.

One of her brothers stepped in front of Quill, holding another stick. Impaled on it was a small round object, charred but dripping fluids. A semicircle of young men formed behind the brother, smiling, nodding their heads.

"Very good," the brother said. "Take it."

"Take it," the young men chorused, poking elbows into one another.

Sam reached across in front of Jane and seized the stick before Quill could get it.

"This ain't for you," Sam said.

He poked it in his mouth and scraped the morsel off the stick with his teeth as he drew it out. He smacked his lips as he chewed and waved his brother-in-law and the other young men away. They looked disappointed.

"That really was good," Sam said. "You'd have maybe liked it, until I told you what it was."

"What was it?"

"Sure you want to know?"

"I've got a strong stomach."

"How about you, Miz Thompson? You want to know?"

"I think so," Jane said.

"Well, them boys was funning you. That critter on the stick was one of the little fellas you see running around in your headlights at night—the critters we call kangaroo rats, though they ain't really rats—all they eat is grass. You poke a stick up their—up their rear ends and roast them whole, like a marshmallow. The hair and hide burns off and what's left is about the tastiest mouthful you ever took in."

"Sorry I missed out on it," Quill said.

"Want I should call the boys back? There's a whole basket of them over by the fire, just waiting to be roasted."

"I think not," Quill said.

The trader laughed. The Klahiako had not appeared, but the heat in the room grew oppressive. Sam Taylor said they had stayed long enough and could leave any time.

"I'll guide you out of the village and then come back here," he said. Quill protested that they could find their way, but the trader insisted. "Nice as most everybody is, you'll be better off with me. Even with no bootleggers here, there's bound to be a few drunks around, and they can get mean. Do senseless things, just like in Gallup."

They followed Taylor along passageways more jammed with people than before, but they saw fewer mudheads and wandering kachinas. The moon was bright, the stars brilliant. They did not realize until the trader had left them and they were outside the pueblo that the wind had died.

"If Sam's right about what a dying wind means, I guess we don't have to worry about witches tonight. They'll have lost their power," Jane said.

"I wonder where the missionary is," Quill said.

Chapter 22

After two days during which the missionary was not seen, the wind started blowing anew, pesky as ever. Once again wind-driven snow veiled the rising sun when Quill rolled up the bathroom window shade, seeking light to shave by. Across the river the pueblo's clay-washed houses looked drab, almost grim, in the haze. Gray smoke from morning fires plumed skyward, only to be torn apart by wind. Shawl-wrapped women, silhouetted against Hawalanee's distant dark bulk, trudged along a snowy ridge toward the river, each with one hand up to brace the water jar on her head. Captive eagles in brush pens beat their wings and screamed at the passing women. Turkey buzzards circled silently overhead, soaring free on fringed wings in the winter sky.

"There goes the water brigade," Quill called down the hall to Jane.

"As many as usual?" she called back from the bedroom.

"Oh, sure. Must be a dozen or more already."

Quill regarded the continued daily procession of even a few Awahi women to the river almost as a personal affront. He saw the wells within the pueblo as his supreme achievement at Awahi. Most women were pleased to draw clear water for household use. But some—even Lina Lituka, or perhaps especially Lina Lituka—still preferred to get their day's first water in the ancient way. They did this though they had to break through ice to reach the shallow and slow-moving rivulets of mud-reddened water.

"Why would the women go to all that trouble needlessly?" he had once asked Jane.

She said, "To fill a void."

To the same question Sam Taylor said, "You know women. They got their ways and ain't fond of change."

Father Aloyisus said, "They're paying respect to their past. Tradition is the glue that holds Awahi together, much as the liturgy does for Christians. For them it is law."

Lina Lituka said, "What you want know for?"

"Just wondered," Quill said.

He was still wondering as he watched the women disappear step by step into a cleft leading to the riverbed, down a steep, twisting trail. Each woman would have to turn sideways to squeeze down the trail, careful of the footing and keeping the fragile pot on her head level. Deerskin moccasins and bulky leggings vanished first from Quill's view, then dark skirt, colorful Pendleton shawl, and at last the crowning water jar, a work of art made in all likelihood by the woman herself.

He peered into the mirror and drew the sharp steel of his grandfather's razor over his cheek. After shaving he stood at the window stropping his razor, sharpening the blade for the next day's shave.

The first of the women came back up from the river. She did not have a pot on her head. Quill did not know what to make of that.

The rest of the women came up, each balancing a pot. They returned to the pueblo in clusters, not the usual single file.

Quill did not know what to make of that, either.

* * *

That evening Jane spooned beans and ham onto their supper plates from a dish that had baked all day in the heat from a banked fire in the coal range.

"Lina was the woman you saw go down to the river with a pot this morning and come up without it," Jane said. "She told me a witch made her stumble and fall and break her pot."

"Who was the witch?"

"She wouldn't say and clammed up all day—seemed really upset. It's bad luck to break a pot, like walking under a ladder."

Someone pounded on the door of the back porch. Quill went out. Before he could close the kitchen door behind him the wind gusted in. The lamp wick flickered and the stove made a loud sucking noise, as though it were drawing cold outside air into the house through a straw.

He was back in a moment, shivering.

"Sam Taylor's oldest boy," he said. "Sam's called a meeting at the post, wants us both there. The little fellow said he didn't know what's up, said it's urgent. I told him we'd be there right after supper."

* * *

Quill and Jane warmed themselves at the flat-topped, potbellied stove in the middle of the bullpen. Quill had removed his mackinaw, but Jane still wore her bulky Hudson's Bay coat. Wind blasted the trading post door open and pushed Father Aloyisus into the bullpen, cloak and habit flaring. He looked like a brown bat in flight, wings beating. The kerosene lantern he carried swung and sent shadows wildly dancing over the walls and floor.

"Well, folks, Father Aloyisus just blew in," Sam Taylor said. "Glad you could tear yourself away from the ladies, Padre." It was an old joke. There were four teaching nuns and an aged housekeeper at the Catholic mission.

Quill checked the time, making a show of it, carrying on another old joke. Still staggering from the suddenness of his entry, Father Aloyisus asked, "Am I late?"

The Reverend Dirk Housma sat on a bench at the side of the

door, upright and stern. "Reverend Aloyisus, you'll be late for the Second Coming," he said, as everyone knew he would. Quill suspected that it might be the only joke the Reverend Housma had ever attempted—a somewhat barbed one, since Housma refused as a matter of principle to call the priest "Father."

"Let me help with that lantern, Father," Quill said. "Don't want it spilling kerosene, or we'll all light up the premises."

He took the lantern and turned down its wick to snuff out the flame. Handing it to Jane, he helped the priest close the heavy door against the wind. Beside one another, Quill and Father Aloyisus looked, as Sam was fond of saying, like a fence post standing next to a brown rock. Jane saw Mutt and Jeff.

Father Aloyisus took no note of Reverend Housma or his remark. To Quill, the two clerics resembled professional gamblers who found themselves thrown together at the same poker table in a strange town. Each knew exactly what the other was up to and up against. Neither interfered with the other's moves or gave the game away.

Dropping his cloak on a bench, Father Aloyisus joined Quill and Jane beside the stove. He dug in the folds of his habit for his pipe, already loaded with tobacco. Clenching the pipe stem between his teeth, he touched the tip of a match to the stove's top. The match flared, and he sucked its flame into the tobacco with a deep breath or two. Emitting clouds of aromatic smoke, he lifted the skirt of his habit to give his trousered backside the full benefit of the stove's heat. Jane would have liked to do the same.

Governor Kenoti and Rain Priest Ninsulka sat on benches facing the stove, Kenoti smiling, Ninsulka looking ready to drop off. Their formal dress—the usual white trousers, velveteen tunics, royal blue for the governor and a rich maroon for the Rain

Priest—along with Kenoti's official cane and massive cross told Quill that the trader had called this urgent meeting on a matter that the two Awahi leaders regarded as serious.

The trader came from behind the counter and hefted the blue-and-white enameled coffeepot that was always warming on the stove.

"Hey, Richard," he called. "Got a fresh pot of coffee out there?"

Richard Lituka lurched through the curtain from the trader's stockroom carrying another oversized coffeepot, identical to the first. He placed it on top of the stove and as always on such occasions returned to the stockroom without looking at or greeting anyone. He took his usual stance on the other side of the curtain. Quill could see his worn-out boots slowly shuffling in place under the curtain as though he were one in a line of masked kachinas in the central plaza.

When everyone who wanted it held a blue tin mug of powerful Arbuckle's coffee, spiked with Carnation condensed milk—Jane had declined coffee, fearful of germs and doubting that any mug once used was ever washed—the trader said, "Let's get started." He said it first in English and then in Awahi.

He turned to Kenoti. "Governor, you want to tell 'em what's up?"

Kenoti aimed his peculiar smile at a pair of cowboy boots dangling from the cluttered ceiling.

"Rain Priest," he said in English.

Ninsulka nodded, cleared his throat, and looked at the four white men in turn—the trader, the principal, the priest, and the preacher. He ignored Jane.

"Trader, he say."

"Well." Taylor took a sip of coffee. "Goddam, that's hot.

'Scuse my French, Miz Thompson, Padre. You, too, Reverend."

He wiped his mouth with the back of his hand.

"The governor and Ninsulka come by tonight right after I closed the post. The wife fixed us a bite to eat."

He put down his cup on the counter beside him and rolled a cigarette, taking his time. He cupped his hands around a burning match and spoke before lifting the flame to the cigarette.

"The governor and Ninsulka," he said, "they tell me—" He broke off to light the cigarette and blew out a lungful of smoke. "They tell me the missionary is dead."

Jane moved close to Quill. He took her hand, held it tight. Father Aloyisus crossed himself. Reverend Housma looked Heavenward. Richard's feet stopped shuffling. No one said anything. They waited to hear more.

"Lina Lituka and a bunch of women went down to the river for water at dawn, like always," the trader said. "Lina comes around that sharp turn right before you get to the riverbed. Before she can stop she steps on something. Her foot slips and she falls down. She drops her pot and it breaks. You all know what that means here—witches and bad luck. And there he is, the missionary, rolled up on hisself, bareass—'scuse me, Miz Thompson—not a stitch on him. Cuts all over him like somebody done taken a knife to him. The governor, he thinks maybe his throat was slit. Dead as a doornail."

"Poor man!" Jane said, pressing against Quill. Father Aloyisus crossed himself again. Reverend Housma kept his eyes fixed on Heaven. Richard's boots shuffled in quick time.

"Anybody at the pueblo know anything?" Quill asked.

The response was what he expected. The governor appeared to smile at the lamp overhead. Ninsulka remained sober-faced, sleepy-eyed. Neither said a word.

"Witchcraft?" Reverend Housma threw the word out as a question. "There's been a lot of talk about the missionary lately."

"What do you think, Governor?" Quill asked.

Kenoti smiled his meaningless smile, shrugged, said nothing.

"Rain Priest Ninsulka?"

"The wind die. Pot break," the Rain Priest said. "Witch."

Kenoti spoke at last. "Witch," he echoed, still smiling.

The word hung in the air. Richard's feet again stopped dancing.

"Sam?"

The trader pondered. "Could be. Or made to look like it. We all know what happens when the wind dies—witch loses his power, that's the time to get him before the wind starts up again. And we all know, like the reverend says, there's been a lot of talk about the missionary. But work him over with a knife? That don't sound Awahi to me."

"Not Awahi!" the Rain Priest declared.

"If somebody cut his throat," the trader continued, "Rain Priest Lituka is right. It weren't no Awahi done it. Sounds more like somebody from the outside. Whoever done it, though, it's murder. And it's a damn shame. Whatever we think of the missionary, ain't nobody deserves to die like that. And what happens next—marshals most likely, maybe the National Guard again—that's a damn shame, too. It's hell to pay and it ain't going to be good for Awahi. Or us."

Quill said, "An outsider—how would he get here in this weather? Anybody seen any strangers around?"

No one had.

"I didn't think so," Quill said. "Whoever did this is right here in Awahi right now."

Chapter 23

They sipped strong Arbuckle's coffee and thought about the wind dying, about witchcraft and the pueblo, about the missionary they had known and what his death might mean to Awahi. And to them.

Richard pushed aside the curtain and came out to shovel coal onto the fire. Quill paced around the bullpen, stepping carefully over Reverend Housma's outstretched legs. Jane studied her fingernails. Sam rolled another cigarette.

Rain Priest Ninsulka muttered something in Awahi. Governor Kenoti nodded. All that Quill caught was "Klahiako."

"What did he say?" Quill asked.

"He says the missionary done a lot of screaming and yelling all over the pueblo during Klahiako," Sam Taylor said. "Says he attacked the Mialosotas, smashed their masks. Serious stuff. Any of you hear about that?"

No one had.

The trader questioned the Rain Priest and governor in Awahi, with an occasional interjection by Father Aloyisus. Mostly Ninsulka answered, sometimes with a comment by the governor. Bit by bit they drew the story out, sometimes in English but mainly in Awahi that the trader translated, with augmentations and clarifications by the Franciscan. The recitation proved time consuming because, in Awahi fashion, Ninsulka needed to start in the distant past. He summarized the missionary's career at Awahi, which had seemed to start out promisingly—hence the grant of land that enabled him to start the Sweet Light of Jesus Mission. Nuisance though he sometimes was, with his shouting and disdainful ways, he often helped people in small ways and paid well by Awahi standards for doing small jobs. ("He was using Reverend Ryenger's money in them days, of course," Taylor added, in an aside.) Ninsulka cited the case of an old widow named Consola Biikiiti, who had no other family and fell on hard times after her husband died. The missionary paid her a dollar a week to clean his shack and chapel. It was enough to support Consola in style.

In English, Ninsulka said, "Then he work for Revenger and fuck—"

Reverend Housma straightened up and opened his mouth to protest.

"Let's not go into that," Taylor said. He added, "There's a lady present."

Housma sat back, arms folded across his chest, alert and wary.

Ignoring the byplay, Ninsulka continued in Awahi, his narrative like a song, a rhythmic and musical recitation of a bill of charges. The trader summarized it in a drone: After the missionary went away to prison and came back, he threw up his crude shelter, brush roof and all, and his little chapel. Over time his hectoring became ever more troublesome. Then came the missionary's attack on the little girl carrying the Virgin Mary's picture, his raids on Awahi's secret caches on Hawalanee, his seizure of the new well, and his interference with the rabbit hunt.

"All the time, bad things," Ninsulka summed up in English.

"Bad," the governor agreed.

Quill pushed himself away from the counter he was leaning against and poured another cup of coffee from the pot on the stove.

"Anybody else?" He held the big pot high. Father Aloyisus took a half-cup. Kenoti and Ninsulka let him fill their mugs. Pouring, Quill asked, "Governor, what do you think?"

The coffee was steaming. The governor sipped carefully to avoid blistering his lips. Smiling agreeably, nodding his head, he twirled a finger at his ear and made a throwing gesture.

"Missionary loco," he said, adding in English, "Since rabbit hunt, loco."

"Loco," Ninsulka echoed. He picked up his story again, recounting how the missionary attacked the Klahiako as they crossed the river, until the mudheads grabbed him, held him down, and stuffed snow in his mouth.

"We saw that," Jane said.

"What more did the mudheads do?" Quill asked.

"Don't do nothing," Ninsulka said. "Let him go."

"What did you do?"

"Nothing."

Ninsulka rolled coffee around in his mouth, swallowed it, and went on. The missionary had wandered the village that night, shadowed by mudheads, shouting his denunciations, doing his tricks, but being mostly ignored by the shivering but festive crowds. In the central plaza just before midnight, with gaiety at its height, he accepted a dish of steaming rabbit stew from a member of his church. He dipped a chunk of meat from the stew with his fingers and instantly dropped the morsel, sticking his fingers in his mouth to cool them. He began scolding the woman who served him the stew, whether for causing him to burn his fingers or for participating in a pagan ceremony was not clear.

The file of Mialosota was passing. Every now and again one

flicked a whip toward a child, inciting much hilarity among watching adults. As they approached, Ninsulka said, the missionary turned and began to berate them in his usual fashion. A Mialosota snapped his whip at the missionary, but did not touch him. The missionary rushed at the Mialosota and knocked him on his back. As the kachina struggled to get up, the missionary poured the steaming dish of stew into the eyeholes and mouth of his mask. The Mialosota shrieked and ripped the mask off. The missionary produced a hammer from under his cloak and smashed the mask to bits.

"I treated a man with terrible burns and a few cuts on his face the morning after Klahiako," Jane said. "He wouldn't say how it happened. He was lucky, though. He could have lost an eye."

Ninsulka went on with his recitation. The unhurt Mialosot a and their mudhead escort rushed the missionary, who fended them off with his hammer, breaking two more masks and bloodying a couple of noses. However, the mudheads, all strong young men, quickly subdued and held him until the kachinas were out of the plaza.

Quill asked again, "What did the young men do then?"

Ninsulka answered in English. "Grab missionary. Take hammer away. Let him go." After all, it was Klahiako. Custom demanded that guests be treated like family. It was not a time for strife.

"When was this?" Quill asked. "Was it when the wind died?"

Ninsulka shrugged, sipped his coffee, and stared straight ahead. Beside him, Governor Kenoti leaned against the bullpen wall and seemed to doze, with the predictable smile on his lips. The silence lasted and lasted.

Finally, Quill asked, "Did anyone see the missionary after that?"

Kenoti came alert and sat upright, still smiling.

"No," he said, leaning back and letting his eyes slowly close.

"Nobody?" Quill asked.

"He mean yes," Ninsulka said.

"Yes," the governor said, nodding his head, smiling, wide-awake and upright again. It was as though the Rain Priest had corrected his English, nothing more.

"Who saw him? When and where?"

"Everbody," the governor said in English. "He all over. Outside, inside. He yell, shake his fist. Loco. He say he look for kiva. Yell, call everbody names, want somebody show him where is kiva. Young men follow. When he get too close to kiva, gods not like. Gods don't want nobody not Awahi in kiva. Too sacred. Gods not let happen—gods keep him out. No one see him after that. He gone. Nobody know where."

"What did the young men do?"

"Nothing. Young men don't do nothing." The governor and the Rain Priest said it together, like a chorus.

They both sat back. The Rain Priest sipped his coffee, stared straight ahead. The governor smiled at nothing.

This time Jane broke the silence. "I've got a question."

Everyone turned to look at her.

"Go ahead," Quill said.

"Why did whoever it was leave the body where the women go for water every morning? Where it was sure to be found?"

The Rain Priest and the governor looked at one another but said nothing.

Sam Taylor translated the question, his usual needless courtesy. Lituka and Kenoti pondered a while, looking not at each other but at the ceiling. Quill sensed, however, that a conference was somehow taking place between them. After several minutes the Rain Priest nodded.

"Young men," he said, "they find him down by river. Dead.

They move missionary where women go. They want people see what gods do when people don't belong try to break into kiva."

Another silence. The Rain Priest and the governor had nothing more to say.

Reverend Housma said, "At least we know who did it."

"And who was that?" Quill asked.

"None of us."

Sam Taylor said, "That maybe ain't going to be as clear to the marshals as it is to us."

"You think there'll be marshals?" Reverend Housma seemed troubled.

"Yep, soon as this gets out. Indians kill a white man? You bet."

Everyone was quiet, contemplating the future.

"Where's the body?" Quill asked.

The trader answered. "At his house. The governor had him carried there and stretched out best they could."

"We should take a look."

"We'll take my car," Sam Taylor said. "It's bigger."

"And easier to start," Quill said.

Father Aloyisus and Quill went out the front door, the priest to take Jenny around to the hay barn in back of the post, next to the stock corrals, and Quill to open the Model T's petcock and drain its radiator. Richard carried hot water to the barn for the Buick's radiator, which had been drained so it wouldn't freeze up. Housma, whose new Essex had methyl alcohol in its radiator and didn't need draining, followed Richard to the barn, along with Jane, the trader, and the two Awahi men.

When everyone was in, it was a big load even for the Buick. The trader drove, of course, with Housma next to him in the middle, his legs wrapped around the gearshift and brake. Quill was also in the front seat, with Jane on his lap. He found her nearness a comfort. Father Aloyisus and the two Awahi men filled the back. Ninsulka and Kenoti balanced primly on the edge of the cushion, clinging to the corded rope that stretched from one side to the other across the back of the front seat. They used it as a lifeline, holding on tightly. They had never ridden in a motor vehicle at night.

When the trader stepped on the starter, the Buick's motor caught instantly—a pleasure to hear, Quill thought. They drove out of the barn and around the trading post, past the Model T and Reverend Housma's Essex. Richard followed on his one-lung Excelsior, seemingly impervious to the wind whipping his face.

Rather than maneuver through the pueblo's narrow alleyways, Taylor took the trail along the riverbank. Quill was surprised that the trader would put his precious Buick over it, but sledges hauling ice and wood had broken up and packed down the snowdrifts and ice that might have blocked it. There were still bumps and ruts, but the Buick's bright lights picked them out in time for Taylor to guide the car around the worst of them.

"Good lights, ain't they?" Taylor said. "Like driving in the daytime."

"My old crate, it's like feeling your way down the road with a candle," Quill said.

After a moment, Taylor spoke again, speaking over the engine's noise, but not loud enough to reach the backseat.

"Damn shame," he said.

"He asked for it in a way, the way he treated these people," Quill said.

"Don't mean the missionary. I mean what's going to happen now. Ranchers, townspeople, and who knows who pouring in to investigate—nice folks, most of 'em, maybe, but wanting to punish somebody, anybody. White man killed! Dirty Indians! Be in all the papers. Get people stirred up, scrapping with one another. I seen it when Richard got tore up like he is. Life's hard enough without that."

"I agree," Quill said. After a moment, barely loud enough to reach past the Reverend Housma to the trader's ear, he added, "But something like this, a murder. Besides this is federal jurisdiction, not state. Local gripes won't matter."

"You're wrong there," Taylor said. "Federal government or the state of New Mexico, it'll be the same folks. There ain't enough government men around these parts to investigate. So they'll swear in the sheriff and his deputies and anybody else they need. Maybe it ain't strictly according to Hoyle, but they'll make it sound legal."

He leaned forward at the wheel to wipe fog off the windshield.

"Long time ago," he said, "a friend of mine owned a post two miles inside the Navajo reservation. His wife come home from a trip to town and found him laying in a big pool of blood and beet juice. The juice come from a can of stewed beets on the shelf behind him that the bullet had went through after it hit him. The bullet was still in the wall. There was tracks of a strange automobile coming and going at the post. Same tracks coming and going in a mudhole right where the road to the post left the highway.

"What Navajo ever owned a automobile? Not one. Them tracks was made by some white man's car. Don't matter. Don't matter neither about the blood, or the beet juice, or the bullet stuck in the wall, or the car tracks. The marshals decided my friend was killed off the reservation and hauled home, which meant it weren't a federal case after all and let them get the case off their hands. The county sheriff found him a couple of Navajos and got 'em to 'fess up to a murder they didn't commit. Hung 'em with state of New Mexico rope."

"They'd have been just as dead with federal government rope," Quill said.

"That's what I'm saying. Federal government or state of New Mexico, it don't matter which when they take after an Indian."

"But somebody was killed in the first place."

"Yeah. And second place, too. Somebody murdered. Somebody found guilty. Federal government or state of New Mexico hangs somebody. Kills him. Guilty or not, ain't that murder, too? Except nobody calls it that."

"But there have to be rules."

"Sure," the trader said, speaking louder now, loud enough to be heard in the backseat, "but the point is, ain't it, whose rules? The Awahis, they got rules—call 'em laws—that they've had since before the Rain God of the North spread his legs and pissed here at Awahi and says, 'This is the place,' just like Brigham Young done a thousand years or so later after he got the Mormons to Utah. Every Awahi knows them rules and knows he's going to get his knuckles cracked if he don't obey them. So now the missionary breaks the Awahi laws and they punish him according to the law—their law. Only now we come in and tell 'em, your rules ain't no good no more. We got new rules for you. So what is it now, this thing that happened to the missionary? Murder? Or enforcing the law? You tell me."

No one answered him.

"Old rules or new? Their rules or ours? You tell me."

Again, no answer.

The trader spoke to Reverend Housma beside him.

"So now the good times is over. Right, Reverend?"

"Over?" Housma asked. "Good times? What good times?"

"Better times than they'll be when we got a lot of nosy outsiders poking around. Federal marshals. Sheriffs acting like marshals."

"Well, these savages killed a white man," Housma said. "We can't stand for that. I for one will welcome an investigation."

Sitting behind the trader, cradling his unlit lantern in his lap, Father Aloyisus spoke up. "Sam has a point. As I understand it, this did not happen because the missionary was white. It happened because he did something that went against the rules by which the Awahi people live and which they regard as laws. And they seem to have taken action against him according to their rules and traditions."

"Not do nothing," Governor Kenoti said. No one seemed to hear his objection.

"What's going to happen," the trader said, "is the sheriff comes in, him and a lot of other newborn marshals with shiny tin stars. They hear this story, that story, another story. They look into them all, everything anybody done, white or Awahi, or that somebody says he done or saw somebody do—everything brought right out on the table. So it ain't just what the Awahi young bucks done or might've done. Now it's also what we done, us folks bouncing along this poor excuse for a road in this here Buick, or more likely what somebody claims we done. We all know not much happens here that somebody don't know about as soon as it happens. Things that don't have nothing to do with this. Even things that maybe didn't happen but got gossiped about. It'll all be listened to. Looked into. I seen it all before."

He turned off the road. The Buick plowed through snowdrifts into the grounds of the Sweet Light of Jesus Mission. Its headlights picked out the pitiful buildings and the small stack of adobe bricks that might someday have grown to make real the missionary's dream of an actual church with four double rows of pews.

Quill noted two fresh paths in the snow leading to the missionary's hovel. One coming from the river was deep and wide, trampled out by many feet. That path was left, he felt sure, by the men who carried the missionary's body home from the river. The other path, though deep, was a narrow track going toward the pueblo—men walking single file through the snow, heading home, carrying nothing.

Braking in front of the missionary's haystack of a house, the trader said, "Case like this, a white man dead, the sheriff or marshal or whoever ain't going to be satisfied just with facts like them two tracks in the snow, one coming in, one going out. He'll want to look into every bit of gossip, true or not, that's floating around. Like, say, somebody in the village'll remember that somebody come home unexpected, not just once, lots of times, different times of day, and he'll remember somebody else saying, 'That fella, he thinks the missionary is fucking his wife'—'scuse me, ma'am—'and he's trying to catch him and her together.' That sheriff with his brand new marshal's star on his chest is going to be mighty interested in nonsense like that. I reckon he'll be asking hisself if that there jealous husband might've been mad enough to kill the missionary."

Housma sat up straight. "What's that you're saying?"

"Just talking, Reverend. Just talking."

The trader stopped with the Buick's lights trained on the missionary's hut.

"Firetrap," he said.

"Disgraceful in the sight of the Lord," Reverend Housma said.

Richard came up.

"One match," he croaked. "Pouf."

Chapter 24

The leather hinges of the jerry-built door had been slashed. When Quill pulled on a hinge the door sagged open, held up only by a padlock. He entered and the others pushed in behind him, Father Aloyisus last. His lantern lighted the room.

Inside, beneath the sagging roof of logs, branches, brush, tar paper, and canvas, unplastered walls of resin-oozing pine logs stacked on one another and chinked with branches and adobe mortar formed an almost circular octagonal room. Resin and mortar had dripped like paint down the logs, streaking them with erratically spaced parallel lines. A small kitchen range stood in the center of the room, its stovepipe rising through the roof, with a wooden kitchen cabinet beside it and a homemade table of rough boards in front of it. The table was unpainted. The cabinet had once been green, but much of the paint had worn away, showing white in some places and pink in others. Its open shelves carried a few utensils and canned goods, as well as folded shirts and underwear. An ancient typewriter and piles of papers could be seen under the half-open rolltop of a battered oak desk. One corner of the desk rested on a length of log in place of a leg.

The missionary's body, covered with the tattered magician's cloak that had come to Awahi with him, lay on a brass bedstead atop the blue-and-white striped ticking of a stained mattress. Quill took a corner of the cloak and pulled it back. The corpse was smeared with mud and dried blood. There were welts and deep cuts all over the missionary's torso and a shallow bloody groove around his neck. The face was mottled red and blue black. The mouth was open, teeth jutting. The eyes were not quite closed. Only a white strip showed between the lids.

"Maybe you better not look, Miz Thompson," Sam Taylor said.

"I'm a nurse," Jane reminded him.

She moved closer, paying particular attention to the marks on his neck. Beside her Richard also looked closely. Nudging her, he pointed to a scar on his own throat.

"Rope," he said.

"Of course," she said. "A deep rope burn. That's what made the governor think his throat was cut."

Kenoti and the Rain Priest stood just inside the door. They heard her but did not speak or change expression.

"Roll him over," she said.

Quill and the trader took hold of the cloak and with a yank rolled the body on its side. The shoulders were hunched toward the neck. The arms had been wrenched back and twisted upward. Deep rope marks encircled his wrists. Most of the flesh had been flayed off his back.

Jane said, "It looks like his arms were pulled behind him, his wrists were tied with ropes, and he was strung up by his arms and whipped."

"Could yucca whips do all that?" Quill asked, his voice unsteady.

He looked at Ninsulka, then at Kenoti. Neither answered.

"You bet yucca could do it," Sam Taylor said. "Ask Richard."

Richard nodded. "Knives, too."

"Richard is right. Knives could do it, too," Jane said. "But I'd guess a flail of some sort. There's so much variation in the direction and depths of the cuts. And there's debris in the cuts that could have come from yucca."

She added, "The poor man must have bled to death. He must have suffered terribly."

Father Aloyisus and the Reverend Housma appeared to be praying. Housma's eyes roamed around the room as his lips moved. Father Aloyisus bowed his head and fondled his beads.

Quill pulled the cloak over the missionary's body.

"Let's look around," he said. "Don't touch anything unless I'm with you. The marshals will want to know who moved what."

The trader was already at the rolltop desk, which looked as though the missionary had found it in a dump. Some of the slats of the rolltop had been smashed and splintered. The desk was covered with stacks of papers and books.

"Something over here," Sam said.

Quill and Jane went to him. A sheet of lined paper torn from a tablet and covered by penciled words in a childish hand lay on top.

"Plese go away stay away," Quill read. "My husban don beleve me. I tell him I have not see you all thees years but he says I lye. Very truly yrs. Mrs. Dirk Housma." There was no date.

He thumbed through more sheets of lined paper. All were the same—illiterate pleas from Mrs. Housma for the missionary to leave Awahi so that Reverend Housma would stop accusing her of being unfaithful.

"Poor woman," Jane said. "Does he have to see them?"

"We'll try to keep them from him," Quill said. He shoved the letters to the bottom of the stack.

In the typewriter was an unfinished letter addressed to the

Commissioner of Indian Affairs, Washington, D.C. It was undated, with many capitalized words. In it the missionary pointed out that Sam Taylor's license to trade on the Awahi reservation was revocable at any time, at the discretion of the commissioner. The letter continued: "I have prevously reported to Mr. John Collier that Trader Taylor is TRAFFICKING in BOOZE but NOTHING IS DONE about this GREVOUS matter." As in the letter to John Collier that Mrs. Olds-Chavez had shown Quill, the missionary proposed that he take over Taylor's trading license, promising to operate a "TRUE CHRISTIAN ENTERPRIZE."

"So the son of a bitch was starting that again," Taylor said. He added, "It still ain't true, you know."

"I know that," Quill said. "But the marshals may not."

"They'll have to see that letter?"

"Yes. Just like Mrs. Housma's letters." He did not realize that Reverend Housma had come up behind him.

"What? What's that you say about my wife?" Housma demanded.

"She seems to have written some letters begging him to go away, saying that you wouldn't believe she had not been seeing him."

"Give me those letters!" Reverend Housma tried to reach around Quill.

"Sorry, Reverend. We can't remove anything from this room. It'll all be part of the investigation."

"What investigation?"

"Of a death under suspicious circumstances."

"Nonsense. It's clear what happened. The heathen Awahis attacked a white missionary who was trying with the fervor granted him by the Lord to draw a godless people from their pagan ways. My wife's letters have nothing to do with it, and I demand that you turn them over to me."

"They'll stay where they are, Reverend," Quill said.

He looked at another stack of letters. "These are about you, Father."

Father Aloyisus thrust his bulk between Quill and Housma.

Quill said, "It's addressed, 'Dear Father,' with a blank for a name to be inserted, but probably intended for one of your superiors. It's like the one to the commissioner that Mrs. Olds-Chavez talked to you about, but it looks like just a draft. Probably hadn't been sent yet."

The Franciscan read the letter. His chubby cheeks suddenly looked rouged, as they had when Mrs. Olds-Chavez told him about the missionary's charges. "Why would he lie so?"

"What's true or not true don't matter," the trader said. "Just saying all this about each of us will mean the sheriff or whoever will have something to dig into about all of us. By the time this is over life ain't going to be worth living."

"I wonder what he was saying about us," Jane said.

"The same things he wrote to John Collier," Quill said. He waved several sheets he pulled from the desk. "He accuses me again of allowing students to speak Awahi in school, which is true, and you of being an abortionist, which isn't."

He put the letters back on the desk.

Jane stared at the paper-littered desktop. "He had his knife out for us all, didn't he?"

"That's right. We're all in this together," Sam Taylor said. "An investigation will just about sink this pueblo—pull it apart. We'll all come under the gun. Don't sound like fun."

"It won't be fun," Quill said. "The papers he left here will guarantee that."

"It's all lies," Reverend Housma said. "Why do we have to leave them here for somebody to paw over?"

"A good point," Father Aloyisus agreed. "We could just bundle all this up and toss it in the stove. Nobody'd be the wiser."

"I'm sorry," Quill said. "I couldn't allow that. It would be tampering with evidence. We'll just have to take our lumps."

As if talking to himself Sam Taylor said, "Fella lived in a firetrap. A missionary dies in a fire? Sad accident, that's all—could've caught from a overheated stovepipe. But a missionary murdered? All hell breaks loose."

He pulled open one of the small drawers at the back of the desk.

"What's this?" he said, holding a silver dollar. He turned it over and found a copper loop soldered on its back. He squinted at it before handing it to Quill.

"That's a loop like was on the good-luck dollar I lost in Gallup when I first met the missionary, twenty years ago. I can't make out the date. Is it 1883? That's the year I was born."

"That's it."

"I'll be damned—begging your pardon, Miz Thompson."

He turned the dollar over and over in his hand, shaking his head. "So that Bible-thumping bastard really did loan me my own money. My own money!"

"I think you can pocket your dollar," Quill said. "Nothing more, though."

He turned to the Rain Priest, who was still standing by the door with the governor. "How about you, Rain Priest Ninsulka? What do you think?"

Ninsulka tipped his head backward and stared up at the jumble of logs, branches, and debris that formed the missionary's roof. He launched into a resonant singsong that sounded like a chant. Again Sam Taylor not so much translated as summarized.

"Ninsulka says white men talk about law, but want revenge. This trouble is Awahi trouble. The white man's way makes more trouble. The Awahi way makes the gods happy and ends the trouble."

Jane asked, "And in a case like this, what is the Awahi way?"

"I reckon that's what Ninsulka is trying to tell us. He says the missionary claimed Awahi gods ain't real gods and anyone who don't believe in the white man God is evil. The missionary don't know nothing about Awahi gods or about Awahi but he yells and calls them names. Ninsulka says the missionary is like a hungry man who eats the seed corn. He don't know you got to plant the seed to get the corn. He don't look ahead to the empty field at harvest time."

The Rain Priest spoke with fire, acting it out, spitting on the floor of the missionary's hut, gesturing. The trader translated in his usual drone. "Ninsulka says that when the missionary spit on Klahiako he spit on Awahi. When he broke the Mialosota's mask he stabbed Awahi. These things ain't what Awahis do—these things is against Awahi law. Leave your gods, the missionary says, come to our God. But if Awahis don't have our gods, who are we? We ain't Awahi without our gods. We're nobody then. We're savages then, like the missionary says. When he tries to kill our gods and treat us like fools and children, Ninsulka says, what can young men do? Die? Or do what Awahi gods and Awahi law say they got to do?"

Ninsulka stopped speaking and pulled his Pendleton blanket across the lower part of his face.

Quill turned to Kenoti. "What do you think, Governor?"

Kenoti also had a blanket hiding half his face, and his voice was muffled. Taylor translated, "He says the missionary was a bad man who did bad things. He paid for bad things he did. Now we pay too."

"But who do you think did this?"

"The governor says it don't matter," Taylor translated. "The missionary's dead."

Quill could not let it go. "It does matter. The man was killed. He was a man no one liked, who maybe wanted to do good but got carried away by the strength of his feelings. Or maybe he was a man who had faith and lost it, a confidence man, a man who hated the world and the people who took his faith from him. What kind of man he was doesn't matter now, because he was a man and he was murdered. That does matter. Somebody killed him. We have to find out who and enforce the law. We have to punish whoever did it."

"That not make missionary alive," Kenoti said. "We got laws. Somebody break laws. We punish our way."

Quill stared at the missionary's body, now only a mound beneath a magician's cloak. He thought about what the governor and Rain Priest had told them and what Sam Taylor in his convoluted way had said about rules and laws and the differences in societies. He thought about Awahi and its people. He thought especially about the ancient culture that the missionary's death would wrench overnight out of its precious isolation into harsh modern reality, without time for people to adapt gradually to the road improvements he knew were in the cards and the telephone line that would soon be strung between Fort Frazier and the pueblo. He thought about the baby Jane wanted and that he wanted, too, but had feared to bring into an uncertain world. He thought about Pine Ridge in South Dakota and the boat-rocking turmoil the investigation of a missionary's murder would bring on Awahi.

His position required him to pursue the missionary's killers and to protect evidence others wished to destroy. But Awahis saw the missionary's death as deserved punishment for transgressing unwritten but ancient rules—call them laws, as the trader suggested and Ninsulka demanded—by which the pueblo had always lived. If the killing broke Awahi laws, Awahi would deal with the killers in an Awahi way. Would it be just for transgressors in a society that lived by one set of rules to be judged by a different set of rules imposed on them by outsiders—rules they had had no part in establishing and of which they had scarcely heard?

Quill had read that New Mexico planned to install an electric chair. He imagined himself in Santa Fe as the lights dimmed all over the city on the fatal night, signaling that young Awahi men were dying for having followed Awahi law. He did not think he could bear it. Change would be inevitable as the world pressed in on the isolated monolith that Awahi had been. But need it be sudden? Need it be now? And which way would better serve justice—the government way or the Awahi way?

Richard stood near Quill, studying the ceiling.

Quill said, "One match."

"Pouf," Richard said.

It echoed in Quill's head. *Pouf.*

* * *

Quill heard loose boards on the bridge pounding under a vehicle's wheels. Jane heard it, too.

"What time is it?"

Quill struck a match and looked at his watch, the watch he still called his brother Ben's, which lay as it always did at night on the bedside table.

"Almost two."

He pulled on his shoes and went to the window. Against the dark backdrop of Hawalanee, the Sacred Mountain, a half-moon bathed Awahi's stacked dwellings with a hint of the golden aura that had so misled the Spanish conquistadores in the sixteenth century. On the far side of the pueblo, a thin column of smoke rose, whipped by wind.

"Looks like Sam's coming to get us," Quill said.

They had been lying on the bed fully clothed except for their shoes. He grabbed his mackinaw. Jane threw a heavy cloak over her shoulders and picked up her nurse's kit. They were waiting on the porch when the trader stopped in front of their house. Father Aloyisus was with him. He had bunked at the trading post overnight rather than put Jenny out in the weather again.

"Got a fire, over to the missionary's place," Taylor shouted, over the Packard's roar. "Lightning, maybe. Or maybe a hot stovepipe touched off all that brush on his roof. Happened to have some barrels of water on this here truck, but don't expect it'll do much good."

"We'll go with you," Quill said. He had put several buckets on the porch earlier. He threw them on the truck beside the barrels of water. He saw that the trader had also brought pails, shiny new ones from his warehouse.

* * *

Blanket-wrapped women with infants in their arms clustered at a safe distance, calling to older children to stay away from the blazing torch the missionary's hut had become. Older boys and men—girls and women, too—formed a bucket brigade with battered pails purchased new at the post long ago, old Crisco lard or No. 10 tomato cans with baling-wire handles, and cowskin pails crafted by their forebears in the distant past. At the end of the line boys and young men seized the buckets and raced through the snow to throw water at the fire, their faces now shadowed and now lighted by the flames. They vied with one another to see who could get closest to the blaze before emptying their pails amid cheers and sometimes cries of alarm. Each bucketful thrown at the blaze raised a small burst of smoke and steam before the fire flared anew.

Jane and Quill found a place in the middle of the brigade beside Lina and Richard and passed buckets with the rest. Father Aloyisus, his frock tucked up to his waist, joined them. The crucifix swinging from his braided belt flashed light from the flames as though sending signals to the stars. Richard dropped out of line to help Sam Taylor dip water from the barrels on the truck.

Reverend Housma drove up in his new Essex with his wife and children. He got out, but the others stayed in the car, doors locked, watching with frightened faces. Mrs. Housma huddled in a blanket with a baby on her lap, her face half hidden. Housma stepped between the crowd and the fire. He held up his hands in a futile attempt to quiet the onlookers.

"Brethren," he shouted, "at this sad time, let us bow our heads and pray the Lord's blessing on our beloved friend, who now sits at the side of Jesus and will be sorely missed by us all." He plowed ahead, his prayer lost in the tumult.

* * *

The hut's roof beams collapsed with a whoosh and a shower of sparks. The juniper logs burned with the vigor of a blaze fresh from the match. The missionary's well was running dry. The barrels on the trader's truck were empty. The bucket brigade gave up the battle.

Quill and Jane stood hand in hand as the walls began to cave in. Over and around the missionary's body an inferno raged. The brass bedstead shone like gold in the midst of flames fed by what looked to Quill like shattered remnants of the missionary's rolltop desk.

As the fire died down Sam Taylor brought Richard to Jane. "Richard's got a splinter," he said.

The splinter was a long one deeply embedded in the meaty part of Richard's palm. His hands were gnarled, rough with calluses. Jane eased the splinter out with tweezers. He did not flinch as she poured iodine on the wound.

"You're a brave man, Richard Lituka," she said.

He lurched stilt-legged to his old Excelsior and putt-putted away with Lina riding sidesaddle on the platform behind him. She waved at Jane and may have smiled. Jane couldn't be sure. Rain Priest Ninsulka and Governor Kenoti shook Quill's hand and nodded at Jane, saying nothing. The governor seemed to smile. Ninsulka looked wearier than ever. The Housmas drove off in their Essex, saying good night to no one. Sam Taylor and Father Aloyisus got in the Packard truck. The trader started the engine. Jane and Quill stood hand in hand, reluctant to leave. The wind was sharp and cold. She leaned against him. He put his arms around her.

"You coming?" the trader called.

"Be right there," Quill answered. To Jane he said, "You know we're stuck here for God knows how long?"

"I don't mind," she said. "I want a baby."

" Here at Awahi?"

"Now."

Washed by the half-moon's pale beam under a starlit sky, Awahi shone against Hawalanee's black bulk as though it might after all be the magical place that Jane, unbelieving, had once glimpsed.